ONE HUNDRED DREAMS

AN ASPEN COVE SMALL TOWN ROMANCE

KELLY COLLINS

BOOK NOOK PRESS

CHAPTER ONE

Cameron Madden sat at her kitchen table, talking to Lucifer. She laughed, because even though she didn't sell her soul to him, Lucifer Abbot, her agent, controlled her life. He had since the day she was born.

"Are you sure Aspen Cove is where I should be?" He recommended the small mountain town to her months ago, and she said yes, but now she wasn't as certain. What did it have that she needed? As if her subconscious was talking to her, she heard the word *everything*.

"Aspen Cove is the perfect place to rest and relax. You might even come back a different person." Lucky, as he was known in the biz because he got some of the best clients, droned on about the benefits of leaving it all behind and embracing something new.

"I don't want to be a different person, but I'd like to be something other than the girl next door."

"You're aging out of those roles, so you'll get your wish soon enough. Let's not worry about the future. Focus on what you need right now."

"All I need is a comfortable bed, a good book, and a latte."

She knew she was one of the fortunate ones, she had a job, and that was saying something in fickle Hollywood where aging out of a career was commonplace. "I need you to find me something that will showcase my skills. I'm more than the ditzy, good girl next door."

"Cameron, I've known you since you popped out of your mother's womb on *The Good, the Bad, and Betsy* set. You came out of your momma smiling at the camera. You are the poster child for girl-next-door movies."

"But I want to stretch my limits. I want more."

"In that way, you're very much like your mother."

She never felt much like her mother. There wasn't much of a comparison in her mind. Beverly Madden was perfect in every sense. She burst on the scene at the same time as Pamela Anderson. While the blonde, bikini-clad babe from Baywatch was awarded the Playmate of the Month, members of the Academy of Motion Picture Arts and Sciences nominated her mother for her second Oscar. It wasn't easy living in the shadow of a great actress. Cameron had been trying to fill her mother's shoes since she was first cast as her daughter in *Bringing Up Amy*.

Too bad life didn't imitate art. There were days when she would have loved to be Amy, a child with magical powers. The best thing about that show was she got to see her mother all the time, and at the end of each show, Amy would take the broom from the closet, and they would ride home. In reality, they'd climb into a limousine and return to their bungalow in the Hollywood Hills, where they'd spend the evening studying the script for the next day. Her mother expected perfection and Cameron was a pleaser.

"What does that have to do with the scripts I get?"

He cleared his throat. "You're naturally suited to roles where the main female character is like sunshine."

"But I can be other things. I don't know why I didn't get cast in *Mean Girls*. I can be a mean girl."

Lucky laughed so hard he snorted. "You don't have a mean bone in your body. You're an anomaly in Hollywood. You're the one they couldn't ruin. Now go and have a good time. Don't think about work or your next role."

"I have to think about it. If I don't, I'll be like my mother, living in Taos, painting abstracts." These days, her mother stood on one side of her home studio and lobbed paint at a canvas and called it art. Fortunately for Beverly Madden, people bought her work. She often wondered why her mother left Hollywood. No one ever gave a reason, but she imagined it was because her mother aged out. There weren't many roles for aging women and rather than accept substandard scripts, her mother left at the top of her game. She announced her retirement on the night she won the Golden Globe Award.

"You could do worse than make thousands for your artistic vision. Now, have fun in Aspen Cove. Frank Arden's house isn't The Residence in Beverly Hills, but I'm told it's a lovely place to relax, reflect, and redefine. There's a lake, a beach, and people who aren't from your world. It will be a nice change of pace. Frank has been a saint moving the reservation around to accommodate your schedule. He was expecting you there weeks ago."

She looked out the floor-to-ceiling windows of her penthouse apartment. "I wasn't expecting to reshoot the love scene so many times." A slight breeze sent ripples across the surface of her lap pool. Living at The Residence in Beverly Hills had its perks. It was like a hotel but without guests, so she didn't have to share her pool. The building even had a spa and room service, but the best part was her doorman, Gary, who never complained when her takeout orders arrived in the middle of the night.

"I meant to ask what happened? The director said you weren't happy with your costar."

"Unhappy is putting it kindly." She opened the door and walked onto the terrace where potted plants lined the walkway. "I wanted to murder him more than once." She smiled at that. "See, I'm not always Miss Sunshine."

In the background, Lucky shook his martini shaker.

She glanced at the sundial, which showed it was two-thirty—well-past drinking time in Hollywood.

"What's wrong with Quintin Nogono? Everyone wants to work with him."

"Do you have an hour?" There were many things wrong with her last leading man.

Lucky laughed. "I do, but you don't. Give me the short list."

The one thing she loved about Lucky was he always had time for her. Cameron never knew her father. According to her mom, she was an angel's gift. Her mother simply woke up pregnant one day. All Cameron could think was the night before had to be a doozy.

Lucky had been the only father figure she knew. Each time she asked him if he was her father, he denied it, but told her if he had a daughter, he'd want her to be exactly like Cameron.

"First of all, Quintin doesn't bathe, and if he does, he doesn't use soap. And when you say love scene, all we're talking about is a kiss and a fade to black because I'm the girl next door and no one thinks I can pull off a steamy scene. But when we climbed into bed, Quintin proved to be a no-go ... no, no, no." She hadn't realized how well his name fit him until that second. "The director yelled cut, and he did just that ... he cut one that cleared the set. I nearly fainted from methane poisoning. Seriously, he has digestive problems. The man stinks any way you cast him." Lucky remained silent, so she continued. "I'm typecast in this truly boring character." Her statement was met with more silence. "I can be mean and vindictive and catty. I can be seductive and murderous, too. Make them give me a chance."

"Honey, when someone steps on your foot, you apologize for being in the way."

"I'm being polite." She huffed and walked back inside her home. Everything was squeaky clean and decorated white. From the walls to the furniture, her style was simple and elegant, but now that she looked at it, it was a blank slate. "I hate that I have this problem."

"What problem?" he asked.

"Invisibility. Nobody sees me. They see what they want. I have no say in my life. Everyone tells me what to do, and I do it. When can I do what I want?"

"Cameron, what do you want? Millions would die for what you have. You're the it girl of romantic comedy."

"I get that." She felt bad for feeling unsettled in her life. She had everything, and yet, she had nothing. "I just want something different."

"To get something different from life, you have to demand something different from yourself."

She sighed. "My life is like a whiteboard waiting for someone to write on it."

"Honey, be your own artist."

"You're right, this is my life, and I'm choosing what's next. No more playing by someone else's rules. I'm done. I don't want anyone telling me what's what anymore." She marched into the foyer and looked at the suitcases her stylist had packed. She didn't even choose her own clothing. Her entire life was like a movie—scripted. "I don't want anyone telling me anything."

"Good for you. Now make sure when Valery comes, you're ready. The Armstrongs aren't known for their patience."

"I'll be ready." She thought about her bodyguard and was grateful they'd chosen a woman. Maybe this Valery would show her a move or two. It would be amazing to get a part playing a badass bodyguard. She closed her eyes and pictured a twist on the original movie with Kevin Costner. Could she be that fearless protector who runs across the stage to save the hero? She believed she could do anything. Too bad no one else did. "I can't wait to meet her."

Lucky choked. "Her?"

"Yes, Valery. That's the name, right?"

Lucky chuckled. "Yes. That is the name."

"Do you think I'll like her?"

"Oh, I think the entire event will surprise you. Take advantage of the freedom and the anonymity. Take this time to figure out what you want your future to look like."

"Do you think anyone will recognize me in Aspen Cove?" She was worried she'd never get a minute's break. The paparazzi were a lens away, and as "America's sweetheart," they were always waiting for her to drop her smile or an F-bomb—two things she occasionally did but had never been caught on film. How could she authentically be herself if she had to be who Hollywood created?

"I have it on good authority that even if they recognize you, the people of Aspen Cove will respect your privacy."

She laughed and snorted. "That'll be the day. The one thing I learned from Mom was privacy doesn't mean private, and the click of a camera is a small price to pay for a penthouse and a driver." That was true, but she still craved moments out of the limelight.

"Do you think your mother's always right?"

She laughed. "Do you want to tell her she's wrong?"

"Not on your life. Have a wonderful trip, Cameron. Enjoy, and be you. Do you need anything from me?"

"Yes, I need a good script." A buzz sounded from the front door, telling her the bellman was calling. "I've got to go. I think my ride is here."

"Good luck with that."

Cameron wanted to ask why she'd need luck, but the phone went dead before she could ask. The buzzer sounded again. "I'm coming." Her words echoed off the walls. Her black heels *click-clacked* across the marble floor. She'd rather be in jeans and a T-shirt, but she knew the press would be waiting downstairs. Her mother had already called and told her she'd tipped them off. That was right before she sent her pictures of the outfit she wanted her to wear—a white Chanel suit with a black and gold belt. Beverly Madden didn't believe that any press was good press. She was of the mind that a woman dressed to the nines got a perfect ten in magazine articles. She glanced in the mirror before she pressed the intercom button. Everything looked picture-perfect, from her false eyelashes to her clip-in extensions.

"Hello, Gary, is my ride here?" She let go of the button and smiled at the mirror, ensuring she didn't have lipstick on her teeth. She hated when she did, and no one told her. She always knew the people who had her back—they were the ones who told her if she had lipstick on her teeth or mascara under her eyes.

"Yes, ma'am. Shall I send him up?"

She stared at the white box on the wall wondering if she'd heard him right. "Did you say he?" She waited for Gary to answer. The intercom crackled, and the doorman's voice was loud and clear. "Yes, ma'am. I have a man from Vortex Security by the name of Valery Armstrong. Shall I send him up?"

She pressed the button. "But Valery is a girl."

Gary chuckled. "Not this one. He's most definitely a man. He's on his way."

Cameron grabbed her cell phone and dialed Lucky.

"I'm assuming you've met Val," he said.

"You knew he was a man, and you didn't tell me?"

He laughed. "Is this the same girl who didn't want people telling her the what's what?"

"You could have told me that. That's critical information."

"What's he look like?"

She hadn't considered what he'd look like because in her mind he was a she, but now that she thought about it, what would a male Valery look like? "I don't know, but I'll find out soon because he's on his way up."

"Oh, I wish I could be a fly on the wall when the elevator door opens. His last client was Georgio Giancomo."

She gasped. "The mafia dude's son?" Her heart rate doubled. "Why would you hire him?"

"He's the best and I only want the best for my clients. See you soon, sweetheart."

She hung up and thought about her dilemma. Off to the side sat her suitcases full of women's things. Things she thought she'd be able to share with her female bodyguard. In her mind, this was like the summer camp she had always wanted to attend but couldn't because it was too risky. In her fantasy, they'd paint their nails and sit outside and share dating stories. This Valery wasn't the Valery of her dreams.

She paced the stone floor and thought about her options as she stared at the floor number on the elevator. She only had twenty more floors before he'd be there. Her natural instinct was to hide in her closet right behind the gown she wore to her mother's final Golden Globe Award-winning ceremony. The layers of pink tulle were full enough that she could get

8

lost in them, and no one would find her. Then she remembered her newfound strength. She was thinking about this
man like he was the boss, but he wasn't. She was the client,
which made her the employer. If he was used to the mafia,
she'd need to dig deep and find her inner gangster.

"Yes, that's it," she said to fill herself with false bravado. "I
make the rules. I decide the trajectory of my life." He
wouldn't be wearing passionate pink nail polish by the end of
the week or sharing first date tales, but he wasn't her boss. As
the elevator numbers rose to greet her, she wondered, what
would Valery Armstrong, a mafia-protecting man, be like?

CHAPTER TWO

Valery Armstrong didn't suffer fools, but he seemed to be surrounded by them lately. As the elevator rose to the penthouse apartment, he took a deep breath and sighed. If it weren't for his last foolish assignment, he wouldn't be in Beverly Hills for his current job—babysitting a movie star. Hands down, he'd rather deal with the mob unless it was Carlo Giancomo's son, Georgio. If not for that particular triple-A fool—an absolute, arrogant a-hole—he'd be doing some other job he disliked a little less than this one.

He watched the numbers rise until he was at the twentieth floor. Five more to go, and he'd have to put his smile on and step into the job he loathed.

Out of his siblings, he was voted the least likely to put up with BS, but that came with a life full of hard knocks, starting with his father's death, which was why he took over Vortex Security at twenty.

The elevator moved past floor twenty-three, then twenty-four, and stopped on twenty-five before the doors opened into the foyer of Cameron Madden's home. She stood there looking more ready for a boardroom meeting than a trip to the mountains. The white suit, black belt, and stilettos blended into the décor, which was also white and black, with hints of gold. He might have missed her entirely if it wasn't for those eyes. They weren't blue, green, hazel, or brown like the average person. Cameron had Elizabeth Taylor eyes—a rare purple color that less than one percent of the population had. He only knew about them because his father had been one of Liz's bodyguards and got to see them firsthand. To his dying day, dad spoke of her eyes like they were one of the wonders of the world. Now that he'd seen something similar, he had to agree with his father. Those eyes were heart-stopping.

As they stared at each other, neither said a word. They seemed to size each other up in the silent seconds that passed until he cleared his throat and offered his hand.

"Hello, I'm Valery Armstrong. You can call me Valery, or Mr. Armstrong."

She yanked on the hem of her jacket and left her fisted hands there. It was as if a string attached to her head pulled her up an additional two inches. As she stood tall and smiled, her fists relaxed, and she smoothed out the wrinkles where she'd gripped the delicate fabric.

"Hello, Mr. Armstrong." She stared at his palm and smiled before she took it. "I thought you might be carrying a gun."

He chuckled. Everyone had a different vision of a security guard, and Hollywood had jaded hers.

"Do I need one?" He lifted a brow in question. "You're not going to give me trouble, are you?" He shook her hand. Was it his or hers that was sweaty? When he let go, they both wiped their palms on their clothes.

"I assure you, I'm no trouble." She glanced down at her outfit as if making sure she didn't soil the fabric. "If it were up to me, you wouldn't be here. Lucifer insisted I have security."

11

"You're a high-value target, and thankfully your agent is wise to protect his investment." This was as good a time as any to set the rules. "As your security detail, I have certain protocols that I must follow to make sure Lucifer's interests are protected." He couldn't believe anyone would name their kid Lucifer and was surprised the man didn't change his name when he was old enough. Then again, he worked in Hollywood, and his name most likely worked in the agent's favor. He couldn't say much; his name was Valery, and he would have changed it if he hadn't been named after his father.

"What protocols?" Her back stiffened as she stared him down.

He pulled an envelope from his pocket and handed it to her. "These are my rules."

She seemed to sink in front of him, but it was a momentary muscle lapse before that invisible string pulled her back up. Only this time, it seemed to drag her forward to stand in front of him. She swiped the envelope from his hand and tore open the flap. Once she drew out the single page with his rules, she let the envelope fall to the floor.

He watched as her eyes moved across the page. Second by second, they grew until he was sure they'd pop from her skull.

She raised her head and stared at him. "Are you serious?"

"Why would I give you that if I wasn't serious?"

"It's a page with one rule. You said rules."

He smiled. "I don't need more than one."

She glanced at the paper and lifted her head. "You make all the rules?" She stared at him like he'd sprouted a horn in the center of his forehead.

"That's my one rule. Take it or leave it."

Her jaw dropped, and she took a step back. "What are you going to do? Leave?" She tore the page in half and let the pieces fall to the marble floor next to the envelope. "You're not the boss, and you don't make the rules."

"Wrong." He turned around, walked back to the elevator, pushed the button, and waited.

"You're seriously leaving? How am I supposed to get to Colorado?"

He took several cleansing breaths before he spun around to face her. "Nothing has changed. You have a flight waiting at Los Angeles International Airport. It will take you to Denver, where you'll have to get a ride to Aspen Cove. Rent a car. It's only a few hours' drive from there to your destination."

She seemed to wobble on her heels. "You're abandoning me?"

He shook his head. "I'm not. I gave you my rules, and you dismissed them. You don't get to be the top private security firm in the country if you break your own rules, and my only rule is I make the rules." The elevator door opened, and he stepped inside. "I'll give you ten minutes to decide. If you're not down in the lobby by then, I'll leave. It's that simple."

She opened her mouth to speak, but the doors closed before she could get a word out.

It didn't take nearly as long to get down the twenty-five floors as it did to go up them. Maybe that was because he dreaded the job, and now he felt free. Little Miss Hollywood seemed like a woman used to getting her way. Most stars did, which was why he loathed these kinds of gigs. He got saddled with the job because Georgio lunged for his father's gun during an argument. There was a struggle, and the weapon discharged. The bullet ricocheted off a metal door and caught Val in the shoulder when he stepped into its path to protect the mobster's son. It wasn't a life-threatening injury. Mostly, it was a flesh wound. But until it was fully healed, it compromised his ability to protect their high-needs clients, and he was stuck babysitting the rom-com queen.

He walked out of the elevator and into the posh lobby on the ground floor. There was a wall of water surrounded by a koi pond. Beyond it was a floor-to-ceiling window where the paparazzi lay in wait. He saw them walking in and knew this job would be a pain in his ass. All he wanted, was to pick up his client, get her in the car, and go to the mountains. Once there, the job would be easy. He didn't see Cameron as a troublemaker. He'd done his job and run a background check on her. For a Hollywood type, she was pretty tame. She had no record. There wasn't a history of drug or alcohol abuse. She seemed to have a level head on her shoulders except for her choice of men and acting roles. Over the last couple of weeks, he'd done his advance work and watched every movie she'd made. That should get him a bonus or a sainthood. They were cheesy romance roles where the character did a lot of blushing and golly shucksing. She was a modern Doris Day. As for her choice of men ... there was a short list of former lovers, including leading men and rockstars. Her go-to was the bad boy, and he wondered if that was her way of shaking off the good girl image.

"Does she need me to get her bags?" Gary asked.

"I have no idea." He looked at his watch. She had a short amount of time to decide if she was staying or going. "I'll be in the car for six more minutes."

Gary had the same look of confusion that Cameron did when the elevator closed. It was a speechless, slack-jawed, confused expression.

Val exited the building to the click of cameras. He was used to this. High-profile people came with bigger-than-life problems.

A photographer jammed his lens in his face and shouted, "Where's the princess?"

Val stopped and looked right into the lens of the camera. With a soft voice spoken with an undertone that suggested he'd disembowel the photographer, he said, "I suggest you move that, or you'll lose it."

The guy stumbled back, tripped over another photographer's foot, and landed on his ass. Val marched past him and climbed into the black Land Rover. She had four minutes to go before he could, with good conscience, put the SUV in gear, press his foot to the gas pedal, and hightail it out of there.

As he waited, he reminded himself of the seven golden rules his father had ingrained in him.

1. Be professional.
2. Respect yourself and your client.
3. Do your advance work.
4. Integrity first—there is no room for ego.
5. Health—take care of yourself, so you're in top form for the client.
6. Develop your skills—one day, they will save a life.
7. Goals—make sure they align with the job.

It was number seven that gave him the problem. He didn't want to be here. Hell, he didn't want to be in the security business at all, but he was the head of his family. He was the V in Vortex, or the second V anyway. He was the oldest of six sons. His father named the company with hopes of filling in the letters. His mother had done her job, giving birth to Valery, Odin, Ramsey, Torren, Easton, and Xander. But then little V popped in at the end. Vivian was an oops baby. His father wanted to name her Sheila so she could represent the S in Security, but his mother said if they did that, she'd have to have seven more kids to finish off the word. She refused and named the only baby girl in the family Vivian, after herself.

To Val, it seemed fitting. They started with a junior by naming him after his father Valery and ended with naming little V after their mother. Vivian was the only girl on the payroll, but if he were honest, she was the biggest badass of them all.

When his minute hand hit the ten-minute mark, he started the engine. Too bad all job cancellations weren't this easy. The crowd of photographers separated as he let off the brake and eased his foot onto the gas. Flashes lit up an already-bright sky, and out of the crowd emerged Cameron. She waved and smiled and stopped at the passenger door.

He wasn't happy, but he was professional, so he killed the engine and climbed out of the driver's seat. He gave her a smile that, on the outside, said, glad you could make it, but his eyes pinned her in place and told her without question that the rules had not changed.

He opened the door, and as she slipped past him into the front seat, he caught a whiff of her perfume, which was sweet and appealing, like those candy shops where the taffy pullers sat in the window, stretching the gooey, stringy glob. He inhaled her scent before he closed the door because he was sure that was the last moment, he'd think anything sweet about Cameron Madden. With those purple eyes and hair like spun gold, she was trouble with an exclamation point.

Gary appeared huffing and puffing, pulling a cart with no less than five suitcases. Val didn't understand why she needed so much, but as far as stars go, she was packing light. He opened the back and helped Gary put the bags inside. All he had was a small duffle. He was wearing a suit, and inside the bag was a pair of jeans, shorts, a couple of extra shirts, socks, and tennis shoes. He believed that what he didn't have, he didn't need.

He said goodbye to the doorman and climbed inside the car. Before he started the engine, he reached behind the seat to where he'd put his computer bag and found the duplicate copy of his contract.

"Before we start, I need to ensure you're on board with the rules." He took a pen from his pocket and handed it and the sheet of paper to her. "All you have to do is sign it, and we're on our way."

She glared at him and gripped the pen so hard he considered it possible she'd shatter the barrel and get ink all over her pretty outfit. "Are you serious?"

CHAPTER THREE

She squeezed that pen so hard she thought she'd crack the plastic casing. "You aren't going to take me until I sign away all of my rights?"

He glanced at the page and then looked at her. His face showed no emotion. His eyes were as lifeless as the dead bug she caught a glimpse of on the windshield.

Outside, the press continued to snap pictures. She had two choices: sit there and argue with him, which only made them late for the flight, or sign the paper and figure out how to sidestep his rule later.

As a flash went off, she scribbled her name on the sheet and shoved the paper and pen toward him. "You know, tomorrow's paper will report this as me signing a prenup or something ridiculous like that."

He put the car in gear, but before he pressed his foot on the gas, he looked at her and said, "Buckle up, buttercup."

She pulled the belt across her chest, buckled it, and they were off. "I thought you were a girl." She watched his profile and how his jaw tightened at her words. "I bet you caught a lot of crap in school for having the name Valery."

He shifted gears, thrusting her forward until the seatbelt snapped her back against the soft leather seat. "It's a family name, and no one would dare give me grief about it."

"Not now, but what about when you were in school?"

He weaved in and out of traffic. "Nope, not then either." His fingers gripped the steering wheel so hard the color left his knuckles. "I was a big kid, and no one messed with me."

"Can I call you Val?"

"Not if you want me to answer. Only people in my inner circle called me Val, and you haven't earned that privilege."

She took him in, from how the top of his dark hair nearly skimmed the ceiling, to how he had to put the seat back to make room for his long legs. He wasn't a hulking man as far as muscle went. He was slim, tall, fit, and crabby.

"How did you get into the bodyguard business?"

"It's a family business."

He obviously wasn't the chatty type, so the next few weeks would play out differently than she'd planned.

"How does this work?"

He pulled up to a red light, stopped, and turned toward her. "I know I'm not your first security detail."

She'd had protection at movie premieres and such, but they were hourly hires who showed up and stayed in the background. At home, she had Gary and the other doormen who didn't let anyone near her without her permission. Mr. Armstrong was different; he wasn't a behind-the-scenes guy, and this wasn't a pay-by-the-hour job. He would be living with her 24/7 for a month.

"You're the first live-in security detail I've had. Do you cook?"

He raised both brows. "I'm not your housekeeper, bellman, or barista. I can cook, and if I'm cooking for myself, I'm happy to cook for two, but that's not my job. Can you cook?"

She lowered her head. "I'm pretty good with eggs." She sat up and smiled. "I'm an expert at take-out."

He made a sound that almost sounded like a chuckle, but there was no sign of it on his face. He was a stoic man. That made her wonder how old he was. A man without expression would age slower than a man who cut it up, laughed, and smiled all the time. For all she knew, he could be fifty with good skin.

"Well, as long as we have eggs, you won't starve."

"How old are you?"

"It's a little late to interview me, isn't it?"

She shifted in her seat. "I'm trying to get to know you."

"There's no point. I'll be here for the next thirty days, and then I'll be at my next job."

She crossed her arms and huffed. "Fine, but you should know about me." She breathed deeply. "I'm thirty-five, but I take care of myself, so I appear younger. I have no major medical problems, and no history of substance abuse." She was proud that she'd grown up in Hollywood and hadn't needed therapy or rehab.

The light turned green, and he gunned the engine as if that would leave the conversation behind.

"Cameron, if we're going to forge a good relationship, then we have to start it honestly. You're not the first woman who has lied about her age." A hint of a smile lifted the corners of his lips, and something magical happened to his face. His hardened expression almost seemed approachable. With a full smile, she might have considered him handsome. "But you are the first woman I've met who made herself three years older. I know your history, from the hospital where you were born, to the day you had your tonsils removed at Cedars Sinai. You have one known scar, and it's on the top of your foot above your right big toe. You dropped a teacup when you were thirteen, and it broke, embedding a piece of fine bone china into the skin. You had five stitches. As for substance abuse, you may not be addicted to drugs or alcohol, but you have a sweet tooth and love orange Starbursts."

She gasped. "How do you know that?"

"I'm very good at my job, and I do my homework." With his right hand, he let go of the steering wheel and reached into his pocket to reveal a sandwich bag full of orange Starbursts.

This felt a little like a trick. The last time someone brought her Starbursts, they also took her for a tetanus shot. "I'm fully immunized."

"Good to know."

"Why did you bring me Starbursts?" She narrowed her eyes.

He lifted a shoulder. "I knew I'd need a peace offering. No woman wants to hear that a man is making all the rules."

"You're right, but let's see how that works out for you." She took the bag, unwrapped a piece of candy, and popped it into her mouth.

"We'll see how not following my rules turns out for you." He grinned, and her heart nearly stopped. Valery had a beautiful smile when he used it. She wondered what kept it hidden and locked up tight. Was it part of the job?

As the fruit chew melted in her mouth, she considered both of their chosen professions. They weren't all that different. He was born into the family business and his stern disposition was part of his uniform. A guy who smiled and chitchatted wouldn't be taken seriously. As for her, acting wasn't a chosen profession but one that was thrust upon her as a child. She didn't know anything different. She'd been born to act. Lucky used to say she came out of the womb with a script in her hand. Her mother swore as a baby she could cry on cue, even before she could speak.

She swallowed her candy and asked, "Did you always want to be a bodyguard?"

"I'm a security specialist."

Weren't they the same thing? "How can you be a security specialist and not carry a gun?"

"I didn't say I didn't carry one. I asked if I needed one. There's a difference." He drove past Los Angeles International Airport to the smaller terminal explicitly built for celebrities. As soon as the Range Rover pulled in front, a team of people rushed out to help with the luggage.

Her door opened, and an older gentleman offered his hand to help her out. "Good afternoon, Ms. Madden. Everything is ready for you."

She glanced at his name. "Thank you, Edgar."

"Do you need a refreshment, or are you ready to board?" The terminal had multiple suites that catered to every need from a masseuse to a manicurist. She was certain they had a good mixologist too. While it was early for her to drink, a martini sounded quite tempting.

Valery walked over carrying his duffle and a computer bag. "We'll board now," he answered.

She turned toward him. "What if I'd like a drink?"

He shifted, so both bags were in one hand. "You can get it on the plane."

"That's right, my trip ... your rules."

He placed a firm hand at the small of her back and guided her into the terminal. "You're a quick learner."

"Top of my class," she said with a broad smile.

"You had a private tutor. You were the only one in your class."

"Like I said, top of my class."

He shook his head. "It's all perspective, I guess."

Valery had a long stride. As he pressed her forward, she

was in a half-run to keep up with his pace. "I don't normally jog in high heels."

"Then take them off."

She came to a dead stop, but his hand at her back kept going, sending her lurching forward.

She tottered but gained her balance. "It's a chartered plane. They aren't going anywhere without me. We can walk at a normal pace."

"This is my normal pace. Contrary to popular belief, the plane doesn't revolve around others' schedules. This airport has to submit flight plans and stick to a timeline. We're already running late because you needed time to adjust to the rules."

She stomped forward. "I hate your rules."

He placed his hand against her back and led the way. "You'll get used to them. They're for your safety."

They walked outside the terminal, where a golf cart waited to take them to the plane. At the chartered jet, he followed her up the steps and entered the posh interior decorated in burled wood and cream-colored leather. Once seated, Valery left her to talk to the pilot. Before she knew it, the doors were closed, and the engine was revving. Valery took the seat in front of her. Mr. Calm, Cool and Cocky didn't look so comfortable. Sweat beaded above his brow, and she wondered if he was warm.

She nodded toward the air vent above, saying, "Turn up the air if you're hot."

"I'm fine." His fingers curled around the armrest and dug into the soft upholstery.

The plane started down the runway. With large jetliners, passengers didn't feel every bump on the tarmac because the weight of the massive plane absorbed the uneven surface, but in a small jet, every dip and divot felt like a major rut in the road. She stared at him and watched him grow pale.

"Are you afraid to fly?" He glared at her, and her hand came to her mouth. "You are, aren't you?"

"I'm not afraid."

The plane sped and lifted into the air.

She turned his rules on him. "If we're going to build a relationship, don't you think we should start it with honesty? You're sweating bullets."

He opened his mouth and snapped it shut so only the thinnest line remained.

"I'm not a fan of flying. I might say, me and airplanes aren't a good mix."

The plane climbed and climbed, until moments later, it evened out, and the flight attendant came to take their drink order. Valery asked for water, and she requested club soda with lime.

"What do you mean, you and airline travel aren't a good mix?"

"Never mind."

She shook her head. "Nope, you can't say something like that and then not explain."

He let go of his death grip and sighed. "I've survived three air emergencies in the last two years."

Her eyes opened so wide a pain shot through her upper lid. Could a person sprain an eyelid? She blinked several times to ease the sharp jab that zipped from her lash line to her eyebrow. "I'm not sure I want to know, but I can't stop myself from asking. How?"

The attendant brought their drinks and left. The staff on private charters rarely got starstruck. If they did, it wouldn't be for someone like her. They'd save their giddy giggles and autograph requests for people like Oprah and Brad Pitt.

"All work-related incidents. One was a bomb. Another was a firearm discharge that caused a change in cabin pressure. The last time was similar but sadder."

Now she was intrigued. "What happened?"

"It was a commercial flight. I was transporting someone's kid from New York to Los Angeles and a drunk passenger opened the door to let their dog outside to pee."

"On a plane? Where was the flight attendant?"

He made a face. "Introducing someone to the mile-high club."

"What happened?"

"We made an emergency landing and my client, and I got on another plane."

She sipped her water and set the glass on the nearby table. "You don't work for very bright people."

"The person who opened the door wasn't related to the assignment." He wagged his finger in the air. "Don't forget I'm working for you. Does that mean you're not so bright?"

"You're not working for me. You're working for Lucky. If you worked for me, you would have been a woman."

"Next time, if Viv is available, I'll ensure you get her."

He smiled, and her world went topsy-turvy. How could a smile change Mr. Grumpy into Mr. Sexy?

"Who's Viv?"

"My little sister, and you should see her rules. You'd probably still be home reading them." He kicked out his feet, leaned back, and closed his eyes. The conversation was over, so she leaned into the wall and did the same.

Sometime later, her eyes snapped open when an alarm filled the air. "What the hell is going on?"

Valery leaned over and tightened her seatbelt before taking care of his own. "Emergency landing. Something is wrong with the plane."

CHAPTER FOUR

He hated flying. What were the odds that he'd survive a fourth air disaster? He gripped the arms of the seat and held on as the plane surged through the air like it was gliding on exploding asteroids.

"Are we going to die?" Cameron's face had lost all of its color. That pretty pink lipstick she was wearing was quickly being chewed off as she bit her lips, probably in an attempt to keep from crying. It was his job to protect her, but there were some things out of his control, and this was one of them. What he could do was comfort her, so he unbuckled his seatbelt and leaped from his chair to the one next to hers before quickly buckling in and grabbing her hand.

"It's going to be okay." He didn't know if that was true, but it was what people were supposed to say, and he followed the rules.

She squeezed his fingers until they lost all feeling. "Are we crashing?"

He glanced out the window, and while they were tottering from side to side, they were still in the air, and not plunging nose-first to the ground below them.

"No, it's a mechanical malfunction of some kind." He looked at the flight attendant, who was the color of a passing cloud, closed his eyes, and made a promise to himself. If they got out of this mess alive, he'd never fly again. "They're trained for this. We'll be fine." It was false confidence because he felt like they'd be anything but fine. What would happen if this was his last moment? Would his family be able to run the business without him? The weight of their lives had sat on his shoulders for over a decade.

Cameron started to whimper. "I'm too young to die. There are so many things I haven't done that I want to do."

She was working herself up to a full-blown cry, and Val knew if he didn't get her to focus on something other than the likelihood of a crash, she'd fall apart before the plane did.

He turned and stared into her eyes. "Tell me something you want to do."

"I want to learn how to drive."

His head snapped back. "You don't know how to drive?"

She shook her head. "It's not easy being famous." She laughed, but it was more like a nervous cackle. "I know that sounds so lame, but I never got to do stuff that others did, like go to prom, and drive a car. I've never been to an amusement park or gone camping."

"I love camping. I always wanted to run an outdoor recreation company." If he hadn't taken over Vortex when his father passed, he would have run a company that specialized in outdoor adventures.

She twisted in her seat to look at him. "Why don't you do that now?"

He pointed to her with his free hand—the hand she wasn't squeezing every drop of blood from with her death grip.

"This is what I do. It's what's expected." The last words his father said to him were, "Keep it together."

"I understand."

He imagined she did. She was brought up in show business and was expected to follow in her mom's footsteps. He got that because his life was the same. Only in his case, people counted on him. With her, she was free to do what she wanted as an adult.

"Do you like acting?"

She stared at him like it was the craziest question in the world. "It's what I do."

He nodded. "I get it, but do you love it?"

"Sure," she said without conviction.

The plane rocked to one side, and the attendant yelped.

"Look at me." He leaned down so Cameron had to look him in the eyes. "If you could do anything else in the world, what would it be?"

She looked around her as if to make sure no one was listening or recording. "I'd open a coffee shop with a lending library, and everyone could come and sit there and read all day. At night, I'd do an open mic where fledgling artists could treat us to their craft, whether it was poetry or guitar or comedy."

"That sounds wonderful. You should do that. Can you make coffee?"

"I make a mean latte." They banked to the left and she held his hand harder. Her knuckles were as sharp as blades, and he was certain he'd be maimed for life from her grip. "You should open an outdoor adventure company. Life is too short not to do what you love."

She was right. "Okay, if we make it out of this, we'll follow our dreams, right?"

She took his other hand and pinned him with her stare. As he looked into her amethyst eyes, he saw that while they were

28

purple, the inner and outer rims of her iris had silver specks that made them all the more beautiful. They were like rare gemstones, and he could spend an hour looking into her eyes and never tire of it. "Now, tell me something else you've never done before."

As they descended, the pilot came over the loudspeaker. "Folks, we're going to have a rough landing, so assume the crash position."

"Head down!" the flight attendant called out.

Cameron folded in half and turned to look at him. He bent over and never took his eyes off her. As they hurled toward the ground, he smiled, hoping to give her confidence that they'd be okay, and if they weren't, he wanted her to leave this world seeing something positive.

"How can you smile at a time like this?" A loud bang came from the back of the plane. "It's probably because you get to die and know what a real, with a human, orgasm feels like." She let go of his hand and covered her mouth. "I can't believe I said that." Her white, pasty complexion turned crimson red. "I'm sorry. Things just come out when I'm nervous."

He gawked at her. "You've never?"

She continued to stare at him. "Yes, I have. It's just been ..." She shook her head and then turned it to the other side. "Never mind."

"Look at me." When she didn't shift to look at him, he said, "Cameron, look at me. My rules, remember?"

She slowly turned to face him. "If we don't die from crashing, I'll perish from embarrassment."

He leaned in until their foreheads were touching. "I signed a non-disclosure agreement. Your secrets are safe with me."

"But now *you* know."

He chuckled. "Chances are, we'll crash and burn, so it doesn't matter. I'll take it to the grave."

"Oh my God. You're awful." The wheels touched down, and the plane whined as the pilot reversed the engines and brought them to a full stop.

She slowly lifted up. "Oh my God ... we made it."

The attendant jumped from her seat and yelled for them to exit the plane. She pushed open the door and an inflatable slide folded out to hit the ground.

He didn't see why they needed to rush until he smelled the smoke and watched it fill the plane. "Time to go." He unbuckled their seatbelts and helped Cameron to her feet. He thought about getting his bags which were just overhead, but he remembered the safety briefing every airline gave. In case of emergency, leave all belongings behind.

"I need my purse," she said.

"No, you don't."

He hoisted her into his arms when she reached for her purse, and he ran for the open door. In one move, he shifted her body, so she was in front of him, cradled in his arms, and jumped. They glided down the emergency slide until his feet were on the tarmac. The flight attendant and pilot followed, and they all ran from the plane. Less than thirty seconds later, there was a small bang and a larger one. Val hit the ground, curling his body around Cameron.

"I got you," he whispered into her hair.

She struggled to see around him. "Did the plane blow up?"

He looked over his shoulder at the flames. "Not yet." Boom! "Okay, yes." He scooped her up and took off to find cover.

"My purse is in there," she said.

"So is my bag."

He ran behind a baggage cart and set Cameron down just as several smaller popping sounds exploded into the air.

"What the hell is that?"

"Ammo."

Her eyes grew big. "Yours?"

He didn't need to answer. She knew. When the bullets stopped exploding, and the emergency vehicles were there putting foam on the fire, he helped Cameron to her feet. "Are you okay?"

She glanced down at her outfit, which was no longer white, but a mix of dirt and tar and whatever she picked up along the way.

"No." Her voice warbled. She lifted her skirt, and he saw her scraped knee.

"You're hurt." He waved to the medic who'd just arrived. "She's injured," he called out.

"It's a scrape," Cameron said. "I'm fine."

"You're bleeding."

He went to touch the injury and she pushed his hand away. "Seriously, I'm okay."

Rather than argue with her, he grabbed her hand and walked her to the EMT, who seemed more interested in the waning fire than he did in the people who needed assistance.

"She needs help."

The guy jumped into action and rushed forward with a medical bag. "I'm sorry. What a crazy situation. Were you on that plane?"

He and Cameron stared at each other and nodded.

"Do you know what happened?" The medic, whose nametag said Aaron, led her to the ambulance and helped her take a seat above the bumper.

"Yes." She pointed to him. "He got on the plane. Every plane where he's a passenger goes down."

Aaron's eyes bugged out. "Is that true?" He cleaned the scrape on Cameron's knee and put a Band-Aid on it.

"It's not every plane but it's the way it's been lately," Val said.

"And you still fly?" Aaron asked.

"Not anymore." He wiped the dust from his suit. It looked grayer than its actual blue.

When he glanced at his client, he realized she was a mess. She was on the verge of a complete breakdown. He needed to get her someplace safe where he could get her a change of clothes and a shower and maybe a drink. Then they needed to make a new plan.

The pilot walked over. "I'm sorry about that. It turns out the cable to the rudder snapped, which caused friction of other parts, hence the fire. We're insured and can replace what was lost."

Cameron sucked in a breath. "I have nothing but the clothes on my back." She reached over and slugged Valery in the arm. "You made me leave my purse behind. I have absolutely zero money or identification."

He rubbed where her knuckles had hit him. Cameron had a punch that would make his sister proud. "That's not true. You've got your life. Don't worry. I've got you." He wrapped his arm around her and tugged her to his side.

"I can have another plane here tomorrow," the pilot said.

"No!" he and Cameron said in unison.

Cameron jumped from her seat at the back of the ambulance and wobbled on her heels. "I'd rather walk."

Val laughed. "Turns out you can run in those stilettos."

"I didn't run, you carried me." She straightened her outfit and brushed her hair from her face. "Make sure no one takes a picture of me looking like this. My mother would never live it down."

He looked toward the building and saw several photographers setting up. "It may be too late." He turned back toward Aaron. "Can you get us out of here?"

It was as if the guy had just figured out who Cameron was. "Wow, you're Cam—"

"Yep, she is. What do you say? Can you give us a lift?"

"The police will want to question you," Aaron said.

"They can call us later."

"Your chariot awaits." Aaron pointed to the ambulance. "Let's go then."

Val helped Cameron inside the back and shut the door behind them. He buckled her onto the gurney and took a seat on the bench across from her.

Aaron climbed into the passenger seat, looked at Cameron and nodded, and then pointed to him. "As soon as you're buckled in, we can go. We've got rules."

"Seems like everyone does these days," Cameron said.

Val was pretty sure using the ambulance as their personal taxi was against the rules, but he wasn't going to point that out.

"Where to?" Aaron said.

Valery looked out the back window and didn't recognize the landscape. "Where are we?"

"Welcome to Santa Fe," the driver said.

He thought about the nicer hotels in the area. He'd been there once, and while he didn't want to stay at the same place he had with Monica, he knew it was the best place to stay in town and he was familiar with the property. "How about The Four Seasons?"

Aaron whistled. "You better have some serious coin."

Val glanced at Cameron, who'd turned on her side to face him. "We can deal with it."

Aaron rubbernecked to see Cameron. "Never mind. I'm

sure you'll be fine." He rubbed his chin. "Would it be rude of me to ask for an autograph?"

"Yes," Val said.

Cameron loosened her belt so she could sit up. "No. I'm happy to sign whatever you want."

The EMTs let out a whoop.

"I'll give you each a hundred bucks if you can get us to the hotel in fifteen minutes," Val said.

The sirens on the ambulance wailed, and the driver gunned the engine.

CHAPTER FIVE

Most people arrived at The Four Seasons Resort in a car or a limousine, but Cameron's life had been over-the-top since she was born. It seemed odd, but fitting, that she came screeching to a halt at valet parking in an ambulance with full lights and sirens. Her mother always told her to make a memorable entrance.

"It took seventeen minutes to get here," the driver said. "I had to take a detour to lose the paparazzi. Do we still get the bonus?" He stared directly at her.

"Don't look at me. I wasn't part of the negotiation. All my belongings burned up in that plane." She wanted to complain, but the truth was, she was grateful Valery grabbed her and ran because if he hadn't, all that might be left were her hair extensions and lashes—both flame-resistant.

"You did well." Valery took his wallet from his pocket and pulled out two hundreds. "I'll call your boss, so you're not in trouble with the detour, and I'll tell him where to send the bill."

Aaron moved from the passenger seat to the back. "Can we take a selfie?"

Cameron stared at him like he'd lost his mind. "Are you kidding me? I just survived a plane crash." She stared down at her soiled outfit and couldn't imagine what her face looked like.

"You don't look any worse for the wear," Valery said. "I'd say, you look..." He nodded and gave her an almost-smile. "Rather attractive."

"If you like roadkill."

Aaron sat on the gurney next to her and leaned in to take a picture before she could say no. "Let me find something you can sign." He rooted through the cabinets.

"Let me see that picture." Aaron frowned but handed her his phone and she had to agree, she didn't look half bad. Inside her nerves were twisted and jumbled, and if she let herself, she'd cry because the whole event was terrifying, but she feared if she let a single tear fall, she wouldn't be able to stop them. "Okay, you can keep it."

He pulled two flat packages of gauze from a drawer and asked her to sign them. She did, making one out to Aaron and the other to the driver, Mike, who'd exited and opened the back door to help her down.

She stood hunched over and smoothed out the wrinkles in her skirt. Valery hopped out and she took both his and Mike's hands to get down. There were a few people who were interested in seeing what was happening. When her heels hit the ground, she smiled and said, "Rehearsing for a part." She pulled her shoulders back and walked past the onlookers, and into the lobby.

Valery caught up to her and leaned in. "You don't go anywhere without me." His hand slid to her lower back and guided her to the front desk.

The girl behind the counter, whose nametag read Tabitha, looked up and grinned. Cameron thought she was in for another selfie and autograph until Tabitha said, "Mr. Armstrong, you're back."

"At least she's not in your inner circle either." Cameron didn't know why it bothered her that she and the front desk attendant had to address Valery in the same way, but it probably had something to do with the way he looked at her when they were crashing. It was as if he cared.

Tabitha looked down at her screen and tapped the keys. "I don't have a reservation for you." She cocked her head. "Unless it's under her name." Tabitha glanced at her without a hint of recognition. "What is your name, and I'll check."

Cameron stared at the woman, and then at Valery. Normally she was the center of attention, but today she was an onlooker, and it felt odd but wonderful at the same time.

"Have you heard about the incident at the airport?" Valery turned and pointed to the nearby bar where an image of the burning plane was on the television screen. "That was us."

Tabitha sucked in a breath. "Oh, my goodness. You must have been terrified."

Cameron couldn't imagine Valery being afraid of anything and watched for his reaction. The only show of emotion was a slight tick in his clenched jaw, but that seemed to come more from annoyance. Then again, he was afraid to fly but didn't seem fazed by the crash. Men were a weird lot.

"We need a place to stay for the night. A suite, if possible."

Tabitha's fingers raced across the keyboard. "I can offer you the Sunset Suite. It's similar to the Encantado Suite you stayed in the last time you visited."

"Perfect," he said.

"I imagine you don't need a bellman." She lifted on

tiptoes and looked over the counter. "But might I suggest in-house laundry?"

"We'll have our clothes ready in an hour."

Tabitha handed him a key and Valery once again led Cameron by placing his hand at the small of her back. She'd never noticed how hot his skin was until that moment; it seemed to burn straight through the fabric of her suit.

"You've been here before?" She looked at him and tried to imagine him staying someplace like this. It had a posh lobby with lovely flowers, silk curtains in southwest colors, and seating that looked like it was the softest leather available to man. "It doesn't really seem like your kind of place." It wasn't that he didn't fit in. In his line of work, he was trained to fit in everywhere, but she couldn't imagine him in golf pants and a polo shirt driving a cart. He had a more rugged vibe about him. She envisioned him in shorts and hiking boots, scaling the side of a cliff. He really should be an outdoor adventure enthusiast. It fit him.

"It was some time ago."

They exited the lobby and walked outside. Her heels clicked on the cement walk. "Couldn't have been that long ago if the receptionist remembered you." They moved down the walkway, past the green and purple flowering bushes and various types of cacti. The contrast between the red dirt and the colorful plants was breathtaking. Cameron could see why her mother loved the southwest. Thoughts of her mother had her heart racing at twice the speed.

"Oh my God, my mother will have seen the news."

Valery stopped in front of a building and passed the key in front of the pad. "It's okay, I sent a message to Lucky and told him you were fine. He said he'd let your mother know. You can call her from the room."

"You told him I was fine? I'm not fine. We almost died in a plane crash."

He pushed open the door and she marched past him into a cocoon of warm colors and lush fabrics. Her shoes seemed to have a mind of their own and took her to the wall of windows that blessed them with a picturesque view of the Sangre de Christo Mountain range.

"We didn't crash, we landed hard. Everything would have been fine if the frayed cable hadn't started some kind of fire."

She kicked off her shoes and dramatically flopped onto the sofa. "Do you think it was sabotage?"

He closed the door and walked over to take a seat across from her. "Do you have enemies I'm unaware of?"

She rolled to a sitting position. "I'm not talking about me. You're the one who dabbles in darkness. All my stuff is sunshine and rainbows." If she were being honest, she had a few enemies, but only because she was successful. Not her mother's kind of successful, but she got a lot of roles others were after. Then again, her consistent employment record had more to do with Lucky's reputation than her skills.

"That didn't happen because of me. I don't make enemies." He shrugged. "Okay, I probably have one, but that's because I didn't step in when Georgio's grandmother beat him with her prized cast iron skillet."

She gasped. "But weren't you supposed to protect him?"

He cocked his head. "It's important to pick and choose your battles. It's more important to know which ones you'll lose. I refuse to go to war with Isabella."

She rose from the sofa and went to the mini bar. She lifted up bottles of still and sparkling water to see if he wanted any. He pointed to the still.

"The nature of your job creates enemies." She walked over and handed him the water and took her seat. She opened her bottle of sparkling water only to have it gush out the top and all over her suit. Today wasn't her lucky day. She rubbed the water into the fabric. She figured if bubbly water helped removed wine, it might be effective on dirt and tar, but she only made things more of a mess. "If someone wants to get to your client, then you become that person's enemy."

"Oh, I let grandma have him."

"I'm not talking about that. I'm talking in general." She pushed her aching back into the overstuffed pillow and sighed.

"Rest assured, this wasn't because of me. It was a simple mechanical failure." He gulped the water and set it on the coffee table that sat between them. "You heard the pilot. It was a frayed cable."

"Okay, what now?"

He looked at his watch. "You need to take your clothes off."

Her eyes opened wide. "Excuse me?" She thought about the secret she'd told him and wondered if he was dead set on solving one of her bucket list items. She had to admit that Valery Armstrong was growing on her, but this wasn't the time.

Valery chuckled and shook his head. "That didn't come out right. I'll need your clothes for when they come to launder them. There's a bathrobe in the closet." He rose to his feet and walked into the adjoining bedroom and came back with a plush white robe. "I'll see what I can do about everything else."

She hadn't had much time to consider everything else, but when she did, a tear slipped down her cheek. It had been a harrowing experience, and now that they'd survived, it was hitting her how close they came to dying.

"Did you think we were going to die?"

He shook his head. "I can't think that way. It's my job to make sure we live."

"Unless your client is Georgio Giancomo."

"Oh, he lived, too." He pulled out his phone and pointed toward the door. "I'm going to plan the rest of our journey. Get yourself comfortable. Lock the doors. Call your mom and don't leave." He turned and walked out.

She finished her water before she took off her outfit and laid it across the back of the sofa. She roamed the suite in her bra and underwear, feeling confident he wouldn't be back anytime soon. It was beautiful with a dining room, living room, and a bedroom. The outside terrace had sweeping views of the high desert landscape, and as the sun set, it cast everything in a warm orange glow.

In the bathroom was a large jacuzzi tub with an equally spectacular view of the canyon beyond. Her body ached and her nerves were fried. What should have been the start of a long and well-earned vacation was a nightmare. She had no phone, no money, no identification. She had one outfit to her name, and it had seen better days. She could only imagine what Sara, her stylist, would say when she learned all the clothes she'd painstakingly packed were gone. It was all too much to take in and so she pushed it aside and ran a bath with bubbles. While it filled, she called her mom.

"Mom," she squeaked out before she burst into tears.

"Oh honey, are you okay?"

She swiped the tears from her eyes and nodded. "I will be. I'm coming to see you tomorrow. I need a hug." They chatted for a few more minutes before Cameron hung up.

Stripping out of her lace underwear and bra, she slid into the luxurious suds, leaned back, and let the heat and scent of lavender transport her to another place. She closed her eyes

41

and thought about pleasant things like ice cream and high thread count sheets and orange Starburst candy.

No matter how much she tried to keep her mind free of the day's events, the memories kept replaying like a movie in her mind. The meeting, the media presence, and the melee of the day's plane disaster. She buried her head into her hands and cried some more. She'd faked a lot of tears in her professional life, but she never allowed herself the privilege of crying for real. Her mother taught her that tears showed weakness and the weak were never successful but at this point, she didn't care.

The click of the door echoed through the suite. "The outfit is on the sofa," she called out, thinking it was someone the front desk sent to get her laundry. She glanced at her discarded undergarments and wished she'd thought ahead to include them.

A tall figure filled the doorway and she instinctively covered herself even though she was buried in inches of bubbles.

"Oh sorry." He stared at her like she was a unicorn dipped in sparkles.

"Do you mind?"

"Not at all. Enjoy your bath." He glanced at the white lace on the floor. "Do you want these laundered?"

In her mind, she was saying yes, but there was no way she wanted him handling her delicates. Her head must have followed her first thought because she nodded without thinking, and he scooped up the tiny pieces of fabric.

"I can take care of that."

He held them out in front of him. "I don't know why you bother. There's not much to them."

She waved her hand in the air. "Go away."

He shrugged and his lips lifted into a little half-smile. "But I brought you a surprise."

"What?" She nearly lifted out of the water until she realized all she wore were water and bubbles and sank back up to her neck.

"I found a cache of Starburst in the gift shop." He walked over and took a single one from his pocket and left it on the ledge of the tub. "I also ordered dinner. It should be here in a few minutes. Lucky said you liked salad."

She wanted to drown herself. She ate salad because it kept her figure where everyone wanted it to stay, but she loved carbs. "Thank you."

"Just because he said you liked salad doesn't mean you're getting one." He turned and looked over his shoulder. "I ordered you a burger and fries because, after today, you need to splurge a little."

If she were braver, she would have emerged from the water like Triton and given him a hug, but if she was embarrassed to have him look at her underwear, there was no way she was letting him look at what they barely covered. On that thought, she wondered if she'd stood in all her naked glory, would he like what he saw? That thought brought her back to him staying at this resort before. "Was it for work or pleasure?"

CHAPTER SIX

"Was what for work or pleasure?" He looked away because staring at her was messing with his mind. It had to be those damn purple eyes or maybe it was the tiny freckles that covered her shoulders. The point was, he was noticing far too much about Cameron Madden. Then again, it was his job to notice everything, but did he have to notice how one of those freckles, the one at the top of her right breast, was shaped like a heart?

"I'm talking about your last trip here. I got the impression you were here with a woman."

He turned back toward the door. "All clients have an NDA, and outside of work, I don't kiss and tell."

"You told me about Georgio."

"No, I told you about his grandmother. He just happened to be part of that story." He glanced at his watch. "Dinner will be here shortly. Next time, close the door behind you."

"Next time, don't barge into the bathroom. Only personal things happen in spaces like this."

He laughed. "You need to live a little. A lot can happen in a bathroom." He shut the door, walked into the living room, and tried to take the image of her shocked expression with him, but all he saw was her skin and bubbles.

He grabbed the bags he brought back from the resort's small boutique and headed into the bedroom, imagining his family's shocked expression if they saw him wearing the banana motif golf pants and a pink polo shirt. They were the only things he found that fit him.

He was able to find a couple of things for Cameron in the little shop in the lobby. He didn't know her exact size, but she was the same build as his sister so he got her Vivian's size, hoping the overpriced jeans and shirt would fit. He had no idea about shoes, so he picked up a range of flip flops and hoped one pair would work until they got someplace where they could buy more suitable clothing.

He was pulling up his banana pants when she walked into the bedroom.

"Oh, my goodness, I'm sorry." She immediately turned away from him.

"It's okay. We seem to be invading each other's space."

With her back turned to him, she leaned on the door frame. "Next time close the door behind you."

He buttoned his pants and tugged on the polo shirt. "Touché. I need to practice what I preach." He slid his feet back into his dress shoes. "It's safe to turn around now."

When she did, she took him in from the tips of his collar to the toes of his dress shoes. Her shoulders shook as she tried to hold back the laughter, but she was failing completely as sputtering sounds seeped from her slightly closed lips.

He stuck one foot out and turned it right and left. "Are the shoes too much?" he asked, trying not to break into a smile.

She walked into the room and then around him. "Oh no, I think the shoes are perfect. They bring out the stems in your bananas." Laughter erupted and they both fell to the bed in a fit. "You should see what I brought you."

She went still before she rose to a seated position. "You brought me clothes?" Her eyes were glued to his pants. "Don't tell me we have matching outfits. I've never looked good in fruit."

He sat up and reached for the bag that had shifted across the bed. "No, you get jeans and a T-shirt."

Her hand went to her heart. "Oh, I love jeans."

He emptied the bag and held up the T-shirt that had a graphic of cactus and a sun. It read I Chose Santa Fe.

"I didn't choose it, but thankfully we're here and not plastered to the tarmac." She took the jeans and looked at their size. "How did you know?"

"It was a good guess. You have a similar build to my sister. I've also got a selection of flip flops in the living room for you to try."

She looked curiously at him. "You know your sister's size?"

He thought about Vivian and smiled. "Her Christmas lists are thorough. She puts her size and the link to the store to buy whatever she wants. Last year she wanted Kate Spade slacks and a pair of leather chaps."

"Kate Spade and leather chaps are hard to imagine together. Then again, I tried to imagine you in golf pants and a polo, and I couldn't, but the universe blessed me with this vision. I have to say, you look—"

"Ridiculous?"

She hugged the clothes to her chest like they were a coveted prize and rose from the bed. "No, it's entertaining. It's exactly how I envisioned you, but louder. They didn't have anything but bananas?"

"They had a pair with pink and green crabs, but the pants only came to my shins."

She laughed. "Good call. I can't be around you if you've got the crabs."

He pointed to her. "Ha ha, you have jokes. Bad jokes. I wouldn't give up your day job to be a comedian."

"Deal. But promise you won't give up yours to be a fashion consultant."

The bell to the room rang and he picked up his soiled suit and headed toward the door. "That's dinner. Get dressed, and I'll wait for you on the patio." He walked out, closing the door behind him.

When he opened the door to the suite, there were two attendants. One to pick up their laundry and one to deliver the food. "We'll eat on the terrace," he said, and the man wheeled the cart past him and outside.

The female smiled. "I'm here to pick up laundry?" She held out a linen bag and he gathered their things and shoved them inside.

"Can we have these back tonight? We're leaving in the morning."

She nodded and told him they'd be back in two hours. He had to admit that money had its privileges. Though he was putting all expenses on the company card, they would be reimbursed by the client. Babysitting Cameron Madden wasn't cheap.

He sat on the terrace waiting for her. She appeared minutes later wearing the jeans, T-shirt, and a pair of the flip flops. In her hand was another pair, the ones with a margarita and paper umbrella pattern. "Did you actually think I'd wear a twelve?"

He shrugged. "I told the woman to give me a pair in every size."

She tossed them to him. "I think these will fit you."

He shook his head. "Do you think they'll match my outfit better than my shoes?"

She took the cloche off the plate. "Perfect."

He didn't know if she was referring to the flip flops or the meal, but it didn't matter. As he looked at her wearing those jeans and that T-shirt, she was perfect. He even loved the way she'd gathered her hair in a bun, and somehow made it stay in place with a hotel pen. Cameron was so much more than he expected.

"I've arranged for an SUV to be delivered in the morning. We can make the trip in about seven hours if we drive straight through."

She picked up her burger which was loaded with cheese and mushrooms and took a big bite. She held up a finger as if she wanted to add something to the conversation, so he waited for her to chew and swallow.

"I need a phone and ..." She rolled her eyes. "Everything else."

He picked up a french fry. "A new phone and your other documents will be waiting in Aspen Cove when we arrive."

"What documents?"

"Things like your ID, your health insurance card, credit cards, and all that kind of stuff."

She gawked at him. "How did you do that?"

"It's all part of what I do."

He took a bite of the almost-cold fries and savored them anyway. He hadn't eaten since that morning, and he was starved. The restaurant could have sent up cardboard with melted cheese and he would have eaten it.

"Thank you. I never thought much about my identification, but without it, I feel like I don't exist."

"Oh, you exist. Besides, you have dozens of movies to

prove you do. They are your legacy. A sort of footprint that proves you were here."

She swirled a fry into the ramekin of ketchup. "Thirty-six to be exact. Have you ever seen one?"

"All of them."

She choked on the fry and reached for her water. "Liar."

"I never lie." He took a bite of burger and felt the grease run down his chin. He wiped it off before it dripped onto his shirt. "Seriously, I watched them all. It was part of the research I did before taking the job."

She stared at him slack-jawed. "You're kidding, right? How awful was that for you?"

He didn't know how to respond, but he always tried to be honest. "It was a long week."

"You're being kind."

He took another bite and nodded. "I deserve sainthood."

"That's not nice, but probably fair."

"It's honest. You play the same girl in every movie. How do you not get bored?"

She sank in front of him. "I do get bored, but apparently, I'm a one-trick pony."

He finished his burger and fries and pushed the empty plate aside. "I don't know anything about acting, so don't take my opinion to heart."

"But you know what you like, and you don't like my movies." Her lower lip turned into a pout.

"Hey, I didn't say I didn't like them, I just thought ..." His mother taught him that age-old wisdom that if you can't say anything nice, then don't say anything at all. "Never mind."

"No, just say it."

"Obviously you're a decent actress, or you wouldn't be as successful as you are. I prefer a little more drama in my movies."

"I want drama. I want to be Kathy Bates and hobble an author. I want to be Kevin Costner and dance with wolves. I want more."

"Then demand more." He'd spent less than a day with her and could see she was a pushover. When push came to shove, Cameron would do what people expected.

"It's not that easy. I'm typecast as the good girl. I'm little miss sunshine. It happens a lot. Look at Angelina Jolie, she's always the femme fatale, or Drew Barrymore, who's the sweetheart. They don't see me as anything but bubbly and nice."

He cocked his head to the side and remembered the fire she had in her eyes that morning. "They've never handed you a contract with one rule before."

"Speaking of rules, you no longer have a contract."

He narrowed his eyes. "Yeah, we do, you signed it?"

"Show it to me," she said.

He pressed his lips into a thin line. "You know it burned in the plane."

She shrugged. "Then it's null and void."

"Cameron," he said in his sternest voice. He'd practiced that voice for years, and it always made his siblings fall in line, but she didn't seem fazed.

"We need to make a detour tomorrow before we head to Aspen Cove."

"No detour." He wanted the first part of this contract to be over, and that was to get her to Aspen Cove.

She lifted her perfectly plucked eyebrows and gave him a sugary sweet smile. The same smile he saw in all thirty-six movies he watched.

"Yes, detour. I've been thinking a lot about the crash."

"Hard landing," he corrected.

"You call it what you want, but my life went up in flames

today, or at least my things did, and I can view it two ways. Either it happened because I got saddled with the unluckiest security specialist alive, or the universe wants me to visit my mother and that's why we crashed in New Mexico. She's in Taos, which is just over an hour away, and I told her we were coming. Do you want to meet my mom?"

Meeting her mother was the last thing on his bucket list, but he'd rather endure that than have her think he was the reason they were sitting in The Four Seasons wearing banana pants and cactus shirts.

"How long do we need to stay?"

"Long enough to hug her and show her I'm fine."

CHAPTER SEVEN

Cameron slept in the bed while he slept on the couch. She couldn't imagine what he'd done with those long legs of his. Did he drape them over the arm or the back of the sofa while he slept?

A soft knock sounded at the door. "Cameron? I've ordered breakfast."

She rolled over and looked at the clock. It was close to nine. "I'm coming." She tossed off the covers and slipped into the jeans he'd bought her before going to the bathroom and brushing her teeth. Her false lashes and hair extensions sat on the counter. As she looked into the mirror, she hardly recognized herself. This was a different Cameron. This was a woman who'd faced a moment of sheer terror, a moment where she thought she'd die. It was a moment that changed her life.

Last night as she lay in bed trying to fall asleep, she relived that alarm and the flight attendant yelling to put their heads down. If Valery hadn't been there, she wouldn't have known what to do. She'd played no parts in her career that had prepared her for that. It was that thought that rocked her world. Her life had been lived through a script. She had no real experiences. Her life had occurred on the set of a movie.

She gripped the hair extensions that lay lifeless on the bathroom counter. Fake. Everything about her was fake.

When she called up Lucky and told him she needed a break to find herself again, she hadn't meant that literally, but it was true. Maybe he knew her better than she knew herself. She'd talked about going to Rome or Paris, and he'd suggested some real downtime—time to be herself. It seemed like a weird suggestion because she'd always thought she was herself, but now that life had dealt her an emotional blow, she realized she didn't know who she was.

She glanced at the blonde hair in her hand and let it drop into the trash can. It belonged to Hollywood Cameron, and she was no longer in Hollywood. She plucked the false lashes from the counter and trashed them too.

After she washed her face with bar soap—she could almost hear her mother gasp—she gripped the counter and stared at herself in the mirror. "Who are you?" she asked. Inside her head, she heard a whisper that said, "I don't know."

She pushed off the counter. "Well, then it's time to find out." She walked out of the bedroom and into the main living area.

Valery sat at the table wearing his navy-blue suit. She would miss those banana pants. They made him seem more approachable and friendly, but now he wore his stern expression and was back in protector mode.

"I took the liberty of ordering a little of everything." He removed the covers from the plates with so much flourish she thought he could be the next top game show host. The new Vanna White, maybe. "There are pancakes and waffles. I ordered yogurt and berries. There's also a Denver omelet." He almost smiled, but he kept those lips contained. "It seemed fitting since we are heading to Colorado."

She took a seat and moved the yogurt and berries toward her. "Did you eat?"

He shook his head. "No, I figured I'd eat what you didn't want."

She looked at the spread and knew she should be good since she ate the whole burger and fries but being good didn't sound good. "I'd like a bite of the waffle too."

He took the Denver omelet and the pancakes. "They're all yours." He pointed to the cups on the table. "Coffee or tea?"

"Coffee, please."

Once they had their meals situated, they ate in silence. The light and airy moments they'd shared the day before were in the past, and he was all business.

"There's a mall nearby. We can stop and get a few things." He glanced at his watch. "I spoke to the police today about the accident, so we are all squared away with that. Once we visit your mother, we'll head north. The keys will be under the mat at the rental in Aspen Cove. Frank's niece has filled the refrigerator with staples, so we'll be okay for a few days when we get there."

"Sounds like you've got it under control."

"It's all taken care of."

She scooped up some berries and yogurt and took a bite, letting the creamy Greek yogurt coat her tongue while the berries popped between her teeth. She picked it because it was her norm. Eat healthy and stay healthy her mother always said. She'd always wondered what chocolate chip pancakes tasted like. She imagined other people ate them every weekend, but she was never allowed because the camera put on ten pounds and now with high definition, the audience saw everything.

"Have you ever eaten a chocolate chip pancake?" she asked.

"Yes, but it's more like a dessert than a breakfast. What about you? What's the worst thing you've eaten for breakfast?"

She thought back to her younger days and smiled. Lucky occasionally would stop by their bungalow on a weekend morning and bring a box of cereal. He almost had her convinced that Lucky Charms were made for him.

"I've had Lucky Charms."

He shook his head. "You were a sheltered child. We're going to have to expand your horizons."

"Promise?" While he was joking with her, she was serious. "I'm in my thirties, and I've never driven anything but a golf cart around the studio. I've traveled the world, but I'm not worldly. I've eaten at the finest restaurants and barely ate."

"Have you ever been fishing?"

She nodded. "I shot a scene at a lake once. I held a pole, and the line was in the water."

"That's not the same. Have you ever put a worm on a hook and felt the line tug when the fish took the bait?"

She let her head hang. "No."

"What about hiking?"

She sat up tall. "I've walked long distances that were quite a hike."

"No, I mean hiked, like in the mountains."

"No, there are wild animals and bugs."

He laughed. "That's the beauty of it."

"Spiders and rodents and ticks aren't beautiful."

"They're part of the natural ecosystem. They all serve their function."

"Tell me what purpose a tick serves but to give people Lyme disease." She moved her yogurt aside and poured syrup over the waffle before she took a bite. The buttery flavor hit her tongue and she swore her taste buds sang.

Valery had eaten half the omelet and was starting in on his pancakes. "Everything has a job. Ticks are a favorite food source for birds. They're an important link in the food chain. They take nourishment from larger animals and transfer nutrients down to lesser organisms."

"Okay, what about bats. They serve no purpose except to terrify people, and they make good Halloween décor."

He finished chewing his bite of pancake while she ate another mouthful of waffle.

"They're excellent pollinators and they spread seeds. They also eat lots of insects which keeps the numbers in check. I recently read an article that said bats eat enough insects to save a billion dollars in crop losses per year. If you like that waffle, thank a bat. He probably squashed an infestation ready to take out the wheat."

"You really do know a lot of outdoor stuff."

He gave her a genuine smile that went straight to her heart. It was funny how some people smiled all the time, and she was never affected, but he only smiled occasionally. When he did, it was life-altering. Maybe that was part of the supply and demand concept. When supply was rare, it was worth more when the product became available.

"In another life, I think I was a mountain man."

"In another life, I was probably a tick." She laughed. Actually, the truth was in this life, she felt like a tick, or more accurately, her career was the tick. It sucked the life right out of her.

She pushed her plate aside and rose from the table. "I'll be just a minute." She looked around for her clothes. "Do you know where my suit went?"

He got up and went to the hall closet. "I put it here." He took the bag-wrapped outfit from the bar. "Are you sure you want to wear it? You might be more comfortable in jeans."

She didn't want to wear it, but she had little choice. "Let me look at it." She opened the plastic bag and sighed. It was a complete mess. "Normally my mom would expect me to arrive looking put together but I'm sure she'll just be excited to see me alive." She pointed to her face. "Is there any way we can stop by a makeup store? I don't want to shock her into an early grave."

"You look amazing. I don't know why you don't go natural all the time. You're beautiful just the way you are."

She got all warm inside from his compliment, but then remembered he was on the payroll. "You're paid to protect me, not flatter me."

"The protection you pay for. The flattery is free and authentic."

She didn't know why that made her feel so good, but it did. "Let me get my flip flops and I'll be ready in a few minutes."

She went back to the master bath and ran her fingers through her hair, then pinched her cheeks to give them a little color, and she was ready.

She knew she probably should have run back and gotten the extensions. They were dyed to match her hair perfectly, and they were high-quality real hair, but she couldn't do it. She'd always disliked them. They might have made her long hair look full and lush, but those clips irritated her scalp. She used to do the weave-in ones, but she couldn't sit in the chair long enough to get them done. It was time to let them go. As she walked out the door to the suite, she had a feeling it was time to let a lot of things go.

CHAPTER EIGHT

Val was never a fan of shopping malls. From a security standpoint, they were dangerous. There were too many places a person could blend in, but from a shopping standpoint, it was a one-stop event where they could both get what they want in a short period of time.

He was glad she stayed in her casual clothes. She drew less attention that way. The Chanel suit and the click-clack of her heels screamed "look at me." While she looked hot in that outfit, it wasn't practical for traveling in a car.

As they passed several stores, he noticed that people's heads were turning. "We need to get in and out of here. I think people are recognizing you already." He took her arm and they slipped into the nearest store. She stopped dead in her tracks.

"What's wrong?"

"I've never shopped for myself. I have a stylist. I have no idea what goes with what. I've got the fashion sense of a gnat."

He sighed. He had no idea either, so he moved them both to the register where a woman stood waiting to ring up the next sale.

"Welcome to Haven, how can I help you?"

Valery pointed to Cameron. "She needs a new wardrobe for a mountain vacation. Money is not a problem, but time is. We need to be out of here in fifteen minutes."

The woman stared at him like he was speaking gibberish. "Perfection doesn't happen in fifteen minutes."

He pulled out his black American Express and set it on the counter. "Maybe not, but this shopping excursion does." He glanced over his shoulder where a group of people gathered at the door, snapping pictures. "Make it ten."

The sales representative whose name was Julie looked at Cameron. "Is he serious?"

She nodded. "He's always serious, but you should see him smile. It's like gazing at a rainbow."

Her comment caught him off guard, and he liked it, but he didn't have time to get distracted. "Can you lock that door?" Val asked.

"Not if I want to keep my job."

He growled. "Fine, she's a size six, and a small on top." He wrapped his arm around Cameron's shoulder. "I need a few things, too. Come with me."

"But what if I don't like what she chooses?"

"You can order what you can't find here from online stores or from Amazon when we get to the property."

He raced through the store and picked up socks, sweats, shorts, and a pair of jeans, along with several shirts and a package of boxers. He'd order his shaving stuff, and have it delivered once they got to Aspen Cove.

"I can't order clothes online."

He looked around and frowned. "Not good enough for you?" They were drawing a crowd which would pose a problem if they wanted to make a quick getaway.

"No, I told you, I don't know how to shop for myself."

They made it back to the register, and he placed all of his things on the counter. "Time to pull up your big girl panties." He remembered the fancy suit and red-heeled shoes. "Who picked out yesterday's outfit?"

"My mother."

"Figures."

"What do you mean, figures?"

"The one thing I'm really good at is reading people and that outfit wasn't something you would have chosen. It has stuffy socialite written all over it."

She stomped a flip flop on the high-gloss floor. "You don't even know my mother."

"I did a little research last night."

She stared up at him with those gemstone eyes. "What? You watched all her movies too?"

"No, I condensed it to press junkets and interviews. She seems very intense."

"She's a mother. All mothers are intense."

He would give her that. His mother was a force to be reckoned with. He swore his left earlobe was longer than his right from the sheer number of times his mom yanked him inside by it.

Julie was arranging outfits on the counter and stood back with a smile. "What do you think of these?"

"She loves them. Ring them up, and I'll pay." He searched the counter. "She needs shoes too."

"Oh, what size?"

"Seven," Cameron said and turned to glare at him. "I'd rather be dressed by a stuffy socialite than an arrogant asshole."

He looked at his watch, and then at Julie. "You've got two minutes. Make it one, and I'll write an outstanding review."

Julie took off at a full run and was back in fifty seconds

with a pair of sandals, sneakers, and loafers. She rang them up, he paid, and they made their way to the front where several fans lay in wait.

Cameron put on her brightest smile and reached for the pen and paper someone was offering. He cut the exchange off with his body. "Sorry folks. It's not her." He pointed to Cameron. "Body double. Do you think Cameron Madden would walk out of the house without makeup?" He shook his head. "Not on your life."

"Oh my God. Makeup. We need to stop," Cameron said as he started forward.

"Everything you need you can get on Amazon." He rushed her past the crowd and out to the car where he all but shoved her in the passenger seat.

When he rounded the SUV and took his seat behind the steering wheel, he started the engine and drove away.

She tugged on the seatbelt and turned to face him. "I can't show up to my mother's looking like this." She pointed to a small purple mark on her cheek and pulled her T-shirt over her shoulder to show a bigger, deeper, purple-colored mark. "If I show up bruised, she'll assume you didn't do your job."

"We're on a timeline."

"Our timeline was shot the moment Quintin Nogono farted in bed."

"What?"

She waved her hand. "It doesn't matter. My timeline was shot weeks ago. Surely, we can stop for makeup. It's a small request when we both know these bruises came from you."

"Me?"

"You can't tackle me to the ground and not have consequences. I have sensitive skin."

This situation was like dealing with his last client's grandmother, Isabella. He wasn't winning so when he saw a drugstore ahead, he pulled into the parking lot. "Fine. They should have what you need."

"Makeup is one thing I know about, and a drugstore doesn't have what I wear, but I'll make do because I'm not difficult or high maintenance."

"Don't fool yourself, you're both."

"I liked you better in banana pants." She swung open the door and stepped out. Instead of waiting for him, she marched into the store.

"Hey, we have rules," he called after her. "You wait for me."

"Don't forget, those rules burned with the plane, but maybe you can order a copy from Amazon since you seem to think they carry everything you need." The door to the drugstore opened and she walked inside and went straight to the makeup aisle. He followed behind with a hand cart. She tossed several items from mascara to blush and lotions inside.

"Do you need so much?"

She stared up at him. "It's trial and error when you're buying a new brand." She tossed in a few more things. "If you would have let me swing by an actual makeup store, I could have saved you a lot of money."

"You could have saved yourself a lot of money. I'll get reimbursed."

"Then why are you complaining?"

She attempted to move past him, but he stood in her path. "Because you don't need all that. You're a natural beauty." She was stunning. More so when she wasn't hiding behind fake lashes and lots of makeup.

"Every job comes with expectations. People expect you to protect them. You have to be physically fit. I bet you can shoot a gun, do some crazy kung fu stuff, and drive a car like the getaway guy who robs banks."

"I can."

"People expect me to look and behave in a certain way. My job is different from yours, but there are still expectations. We have to live our lives in the skin that goes with our jobs. If you'd have shown up a hundred pounds heavier and out of breath from taking the elevator, I would have questioned your skills. I live in a make-believe world of perfection. If I don't look my part, then how am I believable?"

"You want to look believable in your make-believe world?" He needed to stop arguing with her. She seemed to want very little from him. He felt more like a paid travel companion than a security specialist. Though she didn't say it, he wasn't paid to offer his opinion about anything except her safety. That crash had thrown him off his game and he needed to get his bearings back, and fast.

Once they were in the car, she lowered the sun-visor and opened the mirror. For the rest of the trip, she applied makeup and tamed her hair into a ponytail.

The GPS took them to a gated community where they wound around curving roads into the hills. The tall iron gates had a decorative gold B and M embellishment. He knew it stood for Beverly Madden, but he was in a foul mood, and he couldn't help himself from thinking this whole trip was turning into a bowel movement.

"Do I look okay?"

He wanted to tell her she looked gorgeous, but that wasn't his job. "You look like a movie star."

They waited at the gate until a voice on the intercom broke the silence. "Can I help you?" the invisible woman asked.

He pulled out his ID and flashed it for the camera. "Valery Armstrong. I have Cameron Madden here for a visit with her mother."

There was a crackle and silence before a pop came from the gate and the subsequent groan of the motor opening the heavy metal panels. He drove through and wound his way to the front door. Standing on the stone porch was Cameron's mother. As soon as they parked, she ran down the steps and tugged the door open. Cameron was out in seconds and in her mother's arms.

"Oh my goodness," Beverly said. Her hand went to her heart. "You nearly sent me to an early grave. Let me look at you." She stood back, waiting for Cameron to turn in a circle. "Are you hurt in any way?"

Cameron looked at him as if she expected him to answer, but he didn't. This was her story to tell. She shook her head. "A scraped knee and a bruise or two, but I'm fine."

"I'm relieved." Then Beverly narrowed her eyes and frowned. "What are you wearing?" She pulled at the fabric of the T-shirt. "It's not even cotton."

"It's fine, Mom. It's what the hotel had."

Her mother took Cameron's hand and led her into the house. "You could have come here last night. I could have had a whole new wardrobe here by this morning."

As if she just remembered he was there, Cameron pointed to him. "This is Valery. My security specialist."

Beverly was a shrewd woman, and he could see she was sizing him up.

"Do you go by Val?"

"You have to be special to call him that," Cameron said.

"Valery is my given name, and the name I use professionally. I'm named after my father who is deceased."

"That warms my heart. I bet you learned to fight young with a name like that."

"I grew up in a family that fights for a living, so it was fine. Valery is actually a male name that turned unisex. My father's side of the family is French and it's a common name there. Kind of like Shannon is in Ireland. Beverly is used by both men and women in England if I recall correctly." He turned to Cameron. "Your name is traditionally male but is now used for females. Looks like we're flipping gender name norms on their head."

"I've never met a male Beverly." Cameron's mother walked up the stairs and inside the house. "I've asked Hildy to serve us a cocktail on the patio."

"It's only noon, Mom," Cameron said.

Her mother moved her hand through the air like she was swatting at an annoying bug. "That means it's five o'clock somewhere."

As they walked forward, Beverly launched into career counseling, and he got a good idea of what Cameron's life was like. While her mother was obviously loving, she was what he'd call a helicopter parent. He imagined in her line of work, she had to be. Hollywood was unforgiving, and kids left unsupervised got into a lot of trouble. Cameron was never in trouble. For that, he had to give Beverly credit.

"I talked to Lucky and told him he needed to get me different roles."

"That's smart. You can't get one of the coveted names if you're always playing the same girl."

Cameron smiled. "I know, but Lucky won't let me murder anyone."

"What are the coveted names?" Val had no idea what she was talking about but had a feeling he should.

"Oscar, Emmy, and Tony, of course," Beverly said.

A woman came out with a tray of martinis, but he turned it down. "I'm on duty but thank you."

Cameron also passed, telling her mom that her nerves were still frayed from the hard landing.

He placed his hand on her shoulder. "She's being kind," he said. "We pretty much fell from the sky in a crash landing. Your daughter was incredibly brave." Cameron turned her head to him and stared like he'd lost his marbles. "She exited that plane and when she hit the pavement she took off like a racehorse. I've never seen a woman run so fast in Louboutins." He didn't know what kind of shoes she had at the time, but he looked up the red sole kind last night while he was researching her mother.

"Speaking of Louboutins, are you sure you don't want to detour to France? I can get a plane ready in an hour, and we can be at the shops on Les Champs-Elysées by tomorrow."

Cameron sighed. "I need rest, Mom, not a shopping excursion."

Her mother snorted. "According to the news, all your things burned in the plane. I'd say you need a shopping vacation, and what's more relaxing than a day at the spa? We love mother-daughter day. What if we made it mother-daughter week?"

He could tell Cameron was considering giving in and while he shouldn't have cared, he did. They'd experienced something together, and he was proud of the way she behaved.

"I hear Aspen Cove is like Burgundy without the grapes."

"Sounds dreadful," Beverly said.

Cameron sighed. "It sounds peaceful and exactly what I'm looking for."

"Look at the time. Cameron, we really need to get on the road."

Cameron smiled. "He's right, Mom."

"What's the hurry? Can't you stay the night?"

He shook his head. "No, the owner of the house is meeting us to give us the keys. It's important for her security that we don't leave the keys anywhere a person could enter the house without us knowing."

Cameron's head snapped toward him. "Yeah, like under the mat or something." She rose and gave her mother a big hug and kiss. "See you soon, okay?"

"I miss you. Are you sure you don't want to stay? Taos is peaceful and quiet. It's the perfect place to relax."

Cameron hugged her mother more tightly and then stepped back. "I know it is, Mom, but I need some time to figure out what I want, and I can't do that here."

Her mother nodded. "You know I'm very proud of you. You don't need those coveted names to be gold in my eyes."

Maybe he'd judged Beverly too harshly.

"Shall we go?" He followed them out of the house and opened Cameron's car door. When he got behind the wheel, he looked at her. "Are you okay?"

"Yes, I'm fine. Why?"

He started the SUV and drove down the road and through the gates. "It's hard to leave the ones you love."

"It is, but if I stayed, she'd fix everything, and that's not what I need."

"What do you need?"

"That's what I'm about to find out. Aspen Cove, here I come."

CHAPTER NINE

"Tell me the truth," he asked. "Do you love what you do?"

She thought she did until the last picture. "You already asked me that. I have a good life doing what I do. I can't imagine doing anything else."

"Last time you said sure, which isn't really an unequivocal yes. When we were going down in the plane, we made a promise. Do you remember?"

She thought back to that moment and a chill raced up her spine. "We promised to live our dreams, but I'm not leaving my career to open a coffee shop with a lending library."

"Why not?"

"Because it's a ridiculous career choice. That's career suicide."

"I read that your mother paints and sells her pictures for a small fortune."

"That's different from making a cup of coffee. Do you know how many coffees I'd need to sell to earn the equivalent of one of her paintings?"

"I looked at her work. They aren't buying her paintings

because she's good. They're buying them because she painted them. It's kind of like Brad Pitt sculpting these days. I don't know if his work is good or not, but I'd bet people would buy it regardless because his hands crafted it."

"You're probably right."

He turned onto the highway and headed northeast. "What makes you want to own a coffee shop?"

She didn't blurt out the answer right away. She had to taste the words for a few minutes to make sure they were true. She rolled them around her mouth and let them sit at the edge of her lips for a few extra seconds before she said, "I just want something real. I want to make something even as simple as coffee and have it be my creation. I want to make my own rules. I've been living by others' rules my whole life. Even who I've dated has been scripted. But here's the kicker: When I venture out on my own, it never goes well for me."

"Give me an example. Are we talking about relationships or something else?"

"You name it. You did your homework. You've seen who I've dated."

She reclined her seat and turned on her side to look at him. He had a strong profile with an aquiline nose. His lips were full and naturally a watermelon flesh color. Women would die for those lips, but that was the way of nature. It gifted men with long lashes, full lips, and asses that a person could bounce a dime off. Men had it made. Anyone who tells you it's not a man's world hasn't spent time with one. They have regular bowel movements, fall asleep two point six seconds after their head hits the pillow, and they can lose ten pounds by giving up soda. Not every soda, but one a week and the weight falls off.

"You have a thing for bad boys in bands. Were those scripted, or was that you acting out?"

"I wasn't acting out. I was doing research."

"You date for research?"

"I date to see how the other side lives."

"What do you dislike the most about your job?"

She knew exactly what she didn't like. "Lack of freedom. I can't have a normal life at all. Hell, I don't even know how to drive."

"That's right." He put on his blinker and moved to the side of the road. "I think it's time you learned."

She popped up. "Now?" She pushed the button to bring her seat to a fully upright position.

"Why not? We said we'd live our dreams, and one of yours is learning how to drive. There's no better time than the present." He pointed to the door. "Come around and take your seat."

A surge of adrenaline flooded her system. She was both excited and terrified. "Are you sure you want to teach me how to drive?"

"No, so don't take too long to decide."

She couldn't believe it. It was one of the fundamental rights of passage for every American teen, and yet, she'd bypassed it because of her fame. She swung open the door and ran to the driver's side where Valery was getting out.

"Climb in, but don't touch anything." He waited for her to get behind the wheel before he walked around the backside of the SUV. Did he go behind the vehicle because he thought she'd put it in drive and hit him?

When he slid into the passenger seat, he adjusted it for his long legs and turned to face her. "You need to put your seat-belt on."

She tugged it over her left shoulder and buckled it. "You told me not to touch anything, and I'm playing by your rules."

He lifted his brows. "Wow, that's a first."

"Not true. I played by your rules until they burned up and there was no proof of them." She set her hands on the steering wheel. "You asked me what I disliked most about my job? It's what I hate about my life—the rules. I can't live authentically when so many people are watching because someone will have an issue with who I am and what I do. I'm sorry I was a shit when you showed up with your rules, but I'd just made a promise to myself that I wasn't going to play by other people's rulebooks. Then you show up and ten minutes later, I break my promise to myself. It's an endless cycle of me trying to break free, and then someone else yanking me back into reality. The reality is I will never be free."

He reached out and touched her arm. It was like he was giving her strength through his touch, or that's what it felt like as the heat surged past her skin and entered her blood to flow through her veins.

"Let's make a deal. I won't push any rules in your direction unless you're in danger. For the next few weeks, you're going to experience life like an average Joe."

The thought of that made her giddy. "Deal, but what about you? What do you want?"

He looked straight ahead. "I would love to go camping."

She'd never been camping. Her idea of roughing it was going to a place that didn't have an espresso machine or a spa.

"You want me to go camping with you?"

"It is a normal person thing to do."

"It has always baffled me why normal people leave the comfort of their homes and go to the mountains to pee in bushes." She gasped when the reality of that hit her. "Do I have to pee in the woods?"

He laughed. "You can pee in your pants, but I wouldn't recommend it."

She considered it for a second. "What if I'm scared?"

"I once read that if your dreams don't scare you, they aren't big enough."

"This is your dream."

"Not true. You want to be a real boy, Pinocchio, and that means doing average people stuff. Camping is like driving. It's a rite of passage. If you can survive in the wilderness, you can survive anywhere."

She laughed. "Those people haven't been to an audition."

"Leave that all behind. Are you ready to drive?"

She gripped the steering wheel and stared ahead. "As ready as I'll ever be."

"Adjust the seat so your feet can comfortably touch the brake and the gas. Start the engine and put the car in drive. The best way to learn is to do."

"What if I kill us both?"

"Then you'll die happily doing something you've always wanted to do, and I'll still wish I was camping."

She did as he told her and eased on the gas pedal as she pulled into the lane. She got a feel for the road and acceleration and before she knew it, she was cruising along like she'd been driving all her life. She drove for hours as he talked about the rules of the road and reminded her of the speed limit. They stopped in Denver to fill up the tank, and he let her pump the gas herself. It was a silly thing to get excited about, but she was thrilled. What most people didn't realize was the simple act of driving was freedom itself. If she could drive, then she could get in a car and take herself anywhere.

He had no idea the gift he gave her, and she'd repay that gift with a camping trip. He was right, the next few weeks would be spent learning and exploring. She couldn't wait to meet her true self.

Three hours after their stop for gas, she pulled into the town of Aspen Cove. "Wow, it's tiny." Main Street was a blink of an eye with not much more than a bar, a bakery, a corner store, and a diner. Her stomach grumbled as she glanced at Maisey's Diner. "Can we stop and eat?"

CHAPTER TEN

After the first few hours of the trip, he was feeling pretty comfortable with Cameron driving; not comfortable enough to fall asleep, but confident she'd be a safe driver. When they got to the mountains, he planned to take over, but she wanted to keep going and, seeing how driving lit her up, he couldn't say no. Now they were in Aspen Cove and parked in front of the diner. Normally he would have wanted to scope out the place first, but he could see that Aspen Cove wasn't a hotbed of trouble.

"The diner sounds great." He exited and walked around to help her from the car. She stretched and groaned.

"Who knew you could get so sore from driving?"

"It's because you were tense the entire time." She sat stiffly in her seat with her hands clutching the steering wheel and her chin set just above the wheel. She reminded him of a senior citizen who was half-blind by the way she tucked herself close and kept her eyes on the road.

He breathed deeply and caught the scent of pine. "That's the smell of freedom."

She sucked in a breath and said, "I smell bacon."

"That's because you're hungry. Let's go." They walked to the door and when he opened it, a jingle of a bell tied overhead rang out announcing their presence. He glanced around for a secluded table and found an empty booth stuck in the corner on the right side. His security-minded brain kicked in and counted the occupants. There was an old couple in the left-hand back booth, and a group of six at two tables pushed together. A large family with at least seven or eight kids was crammed into a large front booth and a few couples were scattered at various tables throughout.

"We'll take that table," he nodded to the back corner. He always sat so he faced the door, but she slid into his position.

"That's my seat."

She reached for the menu and yanked it from the metal holder. "You've never been here so you can't possibly have a designated seat. Besides, I like to see what's coming."

He stood and pointed toward the other bench. "That's my job, so ... if you don't mind, I'd like to make sure I can do it efficiently."

"We're in a town with a population of about"—she looked around—"twenty-five. I don't see this being the place I have a problem."

"You're fighting me on the rules again."

She smiled. "Because there are no rules."

Rather than fight with her, he took the bench across from her and grabbed a menu.

A woman in white loafers showed up with a coffeepot swinging back and forth. "Hey, kids. What can I get you?"

Cameron looked up. "I'd like a water, please, and tea if you have it."

"Will Lipton do? If not, I got some of that fancy Bigelow brand, but I think the mint's all gone. My Ben has taken a liking to it, and I can't keep it stocked."

"Lipton is fine."

Valery turned his mug over. "I'll take coffee. Is it fresh?"

The woman with a nametag that read Maisey eyed him. "I can't brew it fast enough. Do you know what you want or should I come back in a few minutes?" She poured his coffee and stepped back.

"What's the blue-plate special?" Cameron asked.

In Valery's mind, Cameron wasn't the kind of girl who ordered blue-plate specials. He figured she was the woman who ordered a Cobb salad and asked them to leave everything out but the lettuce and bring the dressing on the side.

"Today, Ben made an open-faced chili burger, served with a fry and onion ring combo. For dessert, we have fresh berry pie." Maisey set her pot on the table and took her order pad from her pocket.

Cameron bounced in her seat like a kid. "I'll take that and instead of the tea, I'll live on the edge and have a real Coke."

Maisey wrote down the order. "Oh, honey, if a real Coke is living on the edge, you need more excitement." She turned toward him. "You need to get your girl out more often. What brings you to Aspen Cove? I can't say we are the mecca of excitement, but we have more to offer than Coke."

Cameron looked like she was a deer caught in the headlights, and she looked at him as if to say, *You answer her.*

"We live busy lives and we're renting a house on the lake for the next month."

Maisey's pen went to her chin. "Frank's house?" Her eyes widened and she smiled. Right then, he knew the rumors beat them there. This was a small town, and in his experience, news traveled faster than a brush fire. He waited for Maisey to set her pad and pen down and ask Cameron for an autograph, but she didn't. She stared at him and said, "What will you have?"

"The same."

Maisey gave them both a last look-over and left.

"Do you think she knows who we are?" Cameron asked.

"I'd bet my banana pants on it."

"You're not really putting up much collateral."

He took a sip of coffee and set his mug down. "Hey, I paid two-hundred and fifty dollars for those pants."

"You paid about two-hundred and forty-nine too much."

Maisey walked past and dropped off Cameron's Coke and walked on by. "We'll see how good Frank Arden's prediction is. He says that the people here might know who you are, but they wouldn't make a big deal out of it." He hated having his back to the room and turned to gather more intel. Maisey was at the table with the large family. He scanned the room and caught a man from the tables that were pushed together staring at Cameron. Something possessive flared inside of him. While he was a bodyguard, he never got attached to his clients, and didn't understand the feeling that settled in his gut. He tried to pass it off as a side-effect of their shared harrowing experience, but in reality, he'd been in several planes that went down, and he'd never had this feeling. If he could place a label on it, he'd say it was jealousy but that was impossible.

When the man rose and started to walk over, his whole body stiffened, and his hands turned to fists. "Looks like the prediction was false. There's a man coming over. I'll take care of it."

Cameron looked up and her face turned pale. "Oh my God. I know him. Play along, please." She ran her hands through her hair and smiled.

"Cameron, what are you doing here?"

The man leaned in and kissed her cheek and Val wanted to punch him.

"Red, it's ... good to see you." By her pause in the middle of the sentence, Val knew she was lying.

"I live here now." He looked around. "It's really quite dreadful, but Samantha married a guy from town, and she moved the recording studio to Aspen Cove."

Red stood and looked at him as if he'd just noticed he was there. "Who are you?"

Since Cameron asked him to play along, he looked to her to explain.

"This is Val, my boyfriend."

Red's head snapped back as if she'd slapped him. Val felt the same, although it was because she called him Val, and he liked the way it rolled off her tongue so easily, like they were familiar. Then again, he was now her fake boyfriend and he supposed she should be familiar. Given they were playing parts, he stood and walked around Red to sit next to his girlfriend.

"Join us if you'd like. It's always nice meeting one of Cameron's friends." He inched over, tapping hips with her to get her to give him more room. She slid to the side, and he tucked in close to her. "Honey, how do you know Red?"

The name sounded vaguely familiar and when put together with the mention of recording studio, he deduced that Red was an old flame—one of those bad boys she seemed to be attracted to.

"We used to date," Red said as he slipped into the seat across from them. "I'm sure she's mentioned me. We almost got married."

Val shook his head. "No, she's never mentioned you." He turned toward Cameron. "Are you keeping secrets, love?"

She gripped his arm and hugged it. "No. Remember, we don't kiss and tell."

She looked at Red and said, "It's better if you leave the past behind. It has no place or purpose in your future."

Val didn't like the way Red looked at Cameron. It was like he was a ravenous wolf, and she was a rabbit waiting to be his next meal. Something inside him reared up and made him want to claim her in front of this man, so he turned, ran his fingers through her hair until he clutched the back of her head, turned her to face him and he kissed her.

She was stiff at first until he traced her closed lips with his tongue. He didn't know if she opened to protest or opened to experience the kiss, but when she did, he delved his tongue into her mouth. She responded with a little squeak and then she turned into him, and her hand went to his chest where she gripped his shirt as if he was going to run away and she was intent on making sure he stayed.

Their tongues danced for seconds, and he soaked in the taste of her. His senses picked up a sweetness that reminded him of strawberries, even though she hadn't eaten one since that morning with her yogurt. When he pulled away, they looked into each other's eyes. He halfway expected to see anger, but all he saw was gratitude and a look of drunken passion. Was that a real reaction or her showing him she wasn't the one-trick pony everyone thought she was?

"Maybe you should get a room." Red cleared his throat. "How long have you been seeing each other?"

The kiss seemed to have left Cameron speechless, so he answered. "We met at work." Since word would get around that he was her security specialist, he figured he didn't have to make anything up. "I started as her bodyguard, and things progressed."

Red looked at Cameron with eyes wide. "You're dating the help?"

Cameron frowned. "He's not the help. He's my soulmate."

Red stared at Cameron as if he were looking for signs of a lie and then his head turned slowly toward Val. "What's your name again?" Red asked.

"You've probably heard of me. My name is Valery Armstrong." He turned to smile at Cameron. "Only she gets to call me Val."

Cameron beamed as if he'd given her the crown jewels.

Red's pupils shifted as if he were looking through page upon page of articles in that tiny brain of his. Then his eyes widened. "The guy who protects the mob?"

Val lifted his hands in a shrug. "It's what I do."

Maisey walked over with two plates and set them on the table. She looked at Red and scowled. "Are you staying or going?"

"I'm going."

She pointed to his table. "Then go and let these two eat in peace."

Red slid from the booth and dragged his feet back to his group. "That one is a pain in the patootie. Sorry he was bothering you. If he won't leave you alone, let me know, and I'll get my cast iron skillet out."

Cameron laughed. "You're like a mobster grandma."

Maisey smiled. "I don't know about that, but I don't have patience for fools and that boy is as foolish as they come." She set their check on the table and smiled. "Let me know if you have room for that pie after you eat, or if you want to take it home with you."

"Will do," Val said.

When she left, Cameron looked at Val. "I get to call you Val?"

"Don't you think you've earned it?"

She nodded. "Why did you kiss me?"

He smiled. "Because you asked me to play along. Why? Did you like it?" He watched a scarlet blush rise up her cheeks.

"For a novice actor, I believe you were quite convincing."

"I'm not looking for an acting career, so as long as you're happy with my performance, then I'm happy." The problem with the kiss was, while his logical self knew it wasn't real, everything felt real. It was like getting a taste of his favorite dessert or meal, and he wanted more. More wasn't an option in this scenario. "Red is going to be a problem. I can see it in his eyes. He's still got feelings for you. What's the story there?"

She squeezed a lake of ketchup onto her plate and picked up a fry. "I don't kiss and tell."

"Today, you do. That man is a threat, and I'm here to extinguish all threats."

She dragged her fry through the ketchup. "He's old history, but if you want to know, I'll make you a deal."

He narrowed his eyes. "Do you think you're in a position to make deals?"

CHAPTER ELEVEN

"Yes, because if you want information, you'll have to barter for it." She scooped up a spoon of cheesy chili and took a bite. Flavors danced across her tastebuds, and they should have delighted her since she loved a good chili, but the only taste that lingered on her tongue was Val, and the kiss he'd thrust upon her. At first, she was shocked, but as the moment lingered and deepened, she was enchanted. She hadn't been kissed that thoroughly since ... never. It was a kiss that made her toes curl, and all her nerve endings stand up and scream ... more, please.

"What do you want?"

She took another bite and made him wait. Her mother always told her the things you had to wait for were more fulfilling. She took another bite and then another.

"Cameron," he said with that dreadful sound that was supposed to make her march to his demands. And while that tone sent shivers down her spine, they weren't from fear. Now that she'd survived a catastrophic life experience, things were bound to change for her. She'd gone through her life being the yes girl because her mother always told her difficult didn't get cast. She was certain her mother hadn't intended for her to be a doormat, but she'd adopted that easy-peasy attitude and while it fit her personality, there were things she wanted from life.

"Does that work for you? You say a single word with a sinister tone and people jump to your bidding?" He moved from beside her to across from her and she felt the loss of his closeness right away.

He slid his plate in front of him and cut into his burger, but before he put the bite in his mouth, he said, "Yes. It always works."

She shrugged. "I almost died in a plane crash yesterday. That's scary shit. Your voice doesn't frighten me. The one thing I learned from the experience is I've had very few experiences." She reached over and touched his hand. "You taught me something valuable yesterday. You taught me that if I don't tell people what I need or want, I'll never get it."

"What do you want?"

It was the second time he'd asked her. "I want information. You know everything about me, and I don't know a thing about you. Isn't that wrong? As your employer, I should have some background information."

"You said I work for Lucky."

"In the end, I'm paying you, so I suppose you work for me."

He frowned. "Is this about The Four Seasons?"

It wasn't only about that. It was about trust and how she blindly accepted that he was the right man for the job. His reputation might have been stellar, and he was great at protecting the mob, but was he the right person to protect her?

"Yes and no. I realize I'm not entitled to information about your personal life, but it seems unfair that you know everything about me, and I know nothing about you."

He took a few more bites and set his fork down. "You're right. And I know what you're getting at. If I want the details about Red, then I need to give you something about me. Is this how you want to play it?"

She thought about that and nodded. "Yes."

He smiled and said, "Monica was an old girlfriend. We went to The Four Seasons as a last-ditch effort to make things work out, and while we were there, she met a hedge fund manager and they left together."

"Did you kiss her like you kissed me?"

He cocked his head as if the question was confusing. "How did I kiss you?"

"Like you were drawing my soul into your being."

"Really?" He took a drink of coffee and set his mug down. "Everything I do is thorough, whether I'm kissing you sense-less, or gathering intelligence on a threat. Now back to Red."

She ate a couple of fries and pushed her mostly-empty plate away. "Before we go to Red, I want to say that Monica was an idiot. I'd never leave anyone who kissed me like that and meant it."

"Monica made the right choice. My job makes it hard to sustain a healthy relationship if I'm traveling all the time. She was jealous of some of my clients. They got to see more of me than she did."

She didn't have to know, but she wanted to know. "How many of your clients have you kissed?"

He smiled. "You're the first."

She grinned and a warm feeling flooded her senses. It was silly to feel so good about being first, but she was also glad he didn't make it a habit of getting emotionally involved with his clients. Then again, what was the point of feeling all warm and fuzzy about a situation that wouldn't ever go past make-believe? She hated to admit that she liked Val and would consider something real with him if they had met under different circumstances, but was he capable of real? In her experience, real was temporary or until they moved on, which in Val's case was his next client.

"I imagine Georgio wouldn't have taken too kindly to you kissing him. How good are you at dodging bullets?"

He took his last bite and shoved his plate away. His hand went to his left shoulder. "Obviously not that good since I got nicked by a stray on my last job."

"Oh my God, you got shot?" She realized when several people turned to look at her, that she'd shouted the words. She leaned in and whispered, "Who shot you?"

"Georgio."

She gasped. "Did you try to kiss him?" She was joking but couldn't help herself. Here was this larger than life, serious man, and while she needed to grow in experiences, maybe he needed to grow too. And one thing she felt he was lacking was a sense of humor. Then again, he did ask if his dress shoes were a good fit with his banana pants, so he had a sense of humor but tucked it away.

"Not on your life. I like my paramours with hair, but not on their faces."

"Maybe you shouldn't be so picky. Look at me, for instance. I don't mind hair on the face. It can be rather sexy."

"Ha ha, now stop stalling. What's the story with Red?"

She sighed and wondered if he was asking from a purely professional standpoint. "We dated."

"Almost married, I heard." He thumbed over his shoulder. "Or says the source."

She rolled her eyes. "Don't you know ... you should never get your news from The National Enquirer or social media." She picked up her glass and took a long drink. She wanted the story of Red to die quickly. "We dated until he slept with the band manager. Red is like a bee and believes he should pollinate all the flowers. What I want is a loyal dog who sticks by my side through thick and thin." She took another drink. "I can understand why Monica left you. You're around rich and famous people all the time, and there's a lot of temptation."

"Trust me, I haven't met a hitman who was hot, yet."

"There's that, but the truth is, your chosen employment would leave a lot of questions in a woman's mind when you're gone. That's the same with rock stars and movie stars. Take me for example. Quintin Nogono is Hollywood hotness according to the masses, and I had to kiss him in my last movie. After each kiss, I ran to my trailer and rinsed with mouthwash, peroxide, and salt water, just to make sure I washed him away."

He sat back and looked at her thoughtfully. "Should we stop by the pharmacy to get you what you need to wash me away?"

She shook her head. "Kissing you was nice, even though you were playing a part. You're a good kisser."

He smiled and her heart did a flip in her chest. "Maybe we should go so I can get your three-ingredient cure."

Her gut clenched. Did he want to wash her from his system? "If you need to get rid of me, that's fine." She'd never questioned her kissing ability, but maybe she should. No one had told her she was a shitty kisser, but no one swooned over them either.

"It's not you, but Quintin. Maybe he's still stuck to that delicious tongue of yours."

She felt like a sunflower in full bloom chasing the sun, and Val was the sun. "Delicious?"

"Strawberry."

"Nope," Maisey said as she approached. "It's berry pie. Do you want it here or to go?"

Cameron patted her tummy. "I'm as full as a tick." She stared at Val, seeing as he was the expert on the insects. All she knew was they'd eat until they nearly exploded, and that was how she felt right then.

"We'll take it to go." He pulled out his credit card and laid it on the table. Maisey swiped it along with their check and walked away. A few minutes later she dropped off two Styrofoam boxes with their pie, and the receipt.

"You ready to go?" Val asked.

A surge of giddiness swept through her. This was her first real adventure in a long time, and she was ready. "Lead the way."

As they walked to the front door, Red stood and stepped into her path. "Where are you staying? Maybe we can get together and catch up."

Val pulled her behind him as if she were in danger. "She's not here to rehash the past," he said in that sinister tone. "She's here to build a future—with me. Step aside."

Red stumbled back. She understood the reaction. Val could be a very hard man and he was intimidating, but she'd seen him in fruit pants and a hot pink polo and that changed everything.

"Take me home, Val," she said as they walked to the car. She climbed into the passenger seat and buckled in. When he sat behind the steering wheel, she said, "I'm ready for the good stuff to begin."

"What has the last day been?"

"An utter nightmare."

CHAPTER TWELVE

He took a left at Lake Circle and went to the second house on the right after the bed and breakfast. The home was on a quiet street and looked like it was built in the seventies with sleek lines and lots of windows—a security nightmare.

He pulled into the driveway and turned to Cameron. "Stay here. Let me get the keys and do a quick sweep of the home."

She was ready to dash with her seatbelt undone and her fingers already engaged with the door latch. "Do you really think someone is lying in wait? I'm two weeks behind schedule." She giggled and let her hand drop to her lap. "They would have starved by now if they've been hiding in the house the whole time."

"Not true. Frank's niece stocked the refrigerator."

"True, but I think it will be fine."

"I'm not taking any chances." He stepped out of the SUV, then closed and locked the door. He made his way to the front step and found the keys exactly where Frank said they'd be, under the welcome mat. In the corner were several packages, no doubt Cameron's documents, and her phone. It was a surprise that no one had stolen them.

When he was doing his background work, he'd called the sheriff and asked about the crime rate in Aspen Cove. Outside of a few teenage shenanigans, there didn't seem to be much going on. Sheriff Cooper said that people didn't even lock their houses which was a foreign concept to Val. He spent equal time on both coasts. California and New York were places you not only locked your door but had full security systems. Regardless of perceived safety, crime had no address, and he never let his guard down.

He walked inside the house and breathed in the scent of lemon oil. The hardwood floors shined like glass, and the floor-to-ceiling windows showcased the most magnificent view of the lake. He stared at the slow lap of the water that washed onto the shore. It was early fall, and the fishermen were still on the lake. It's where he would be if he wasn't working all the time. He moved through the house. Thankfully it was small, with only two bedrooms, two bathrooms, a living room, and kitchen. It would be easy to secure. He knew Cameron was right, there wouldn't be any trouble in Aspen Cove unless her old boyfriend decided to create some.

As he walked back into the living room, he caught sight of blonde hair and blue jeans.

"What the hell?" He marched to the door that led to the deck and stepped outside. "You're supposed to be waiting in the car."

She put her fingers to her lips and pointed to a nearby tree. "Look, it's a family of moose."

He looked to where she pointed and found a bull elk and his harem. Cameron needed to get out more if she thought that was a moose. He wanted to be angry at her for not doing what he said, but he understood what drew her out of the car. The animals were a majestic sight to see.

She continued to inch toward them. "I wish I had my phone," she whispered.

"Don't get too close. It's coming up on rutting season, and the big bull will be protective of his harem." He walked down the steps to lead her away from the group of elk eating leaves and drinking water.

"Harem? You mean all those females are his?"

"Elk usually stick to same-sex groups but during mating season they'll separate and form a harem with one dominant male and several females."

"He reminds me of a few musicians I know. One man and a bunch of women." She walked up the steps and leaned on the rail, still staring at the animals by the water. She pointed to one female who stood out from the rest. "I bet she has the big guy eating out of her hand."

"You mean her hoof?"

"If I had to go back to Hollywood tomorrow, just seeing that was worth everything we had to go through to get here." She glanced at the herd, which had moved farther up the shore. She kicked off the rail and walked into the house. "So, this is home, huh?"

"It's not smart to get too close to things that can hurt you."

"Don't I know it." She walked around the living room which had a large sofa that sat in front of the window. Off to the right was a fireplace that was flanked by a couple of leather chairs. Next to the living room was a small kitchen that seemed to have everything from wine to a Keurig. He followed her down the hallway where she peeked her head into both rooms. "Which bedroom do you want?"

It was sweet of her to ask given that she was paying for the place. He would have liked to put her in the smaller bedroom only because it didn't have a sliding glass door that opened to a small deck that overlooked the lake, but he knew she'd appreciate the en suite bathroom and the view.

"I'll take the small room. This is your vacation, and you should enjoy what the house has to offer." Taking the smaller room did have advantages. She'd have to pass by his room to leave. Since she seemed hellbent on breaking all the rules, that seemed like a good place for him to camp out. "Should we go over the rules again?"

She turned, kicked out a hip, and sighed. "Are we going to go over this again? There are no rules."

"The rules are designed to keep you safe."

"Give me one sensible rule, and I'll decide if I'm following it."

There were lots that he could recite from memory but the only one that came to mind was, "Don't play with fire." It was probably because kissing her at the diner felt like he was doing just that.

She smiled. "Done, are you happy?"

"It's a start. Now tell me about your bull elk."

"My what?"

"You compared that beautiful beast out there to a musician. There's a story there I'd like to know."

She walked back into her room, kicked off her shoes, and flopped onto the bed. The large king nearly swallowed her whole.

"Come join me. I thought I was getting Valery the girl and swapping stories was part of the plan." She scooted up so her head was on the pillow, and then she patted the mattress beside her. "Don't worry, I won't ask you to paint my toenails."

He stared at the bed and then her. The last place he wanted to be was on a mattress with Cameron. That wasn't true but being in bed with Cameron wasn't a smart move. He'd already kissed her as part of a ploy, and he enjoyed it far more than he wanted to admit. Her lips were soft as silk, and she tasted sweet like fresh berries. She gripped his shirt like she never wanted to leave and that did something to his heart. He was still trying to figure out why he'd kissed her. It was a primal instinct. In that moment he felt like a bull elk ready to clash antlers with Red. He'd never felt like this with any of his clients, but ever since he'd stepped off that elevator and into Cameron's penthouse, nothing had gone as he planned.

"Come on." She shifted and half-bounced on the bedspread. "It's surprisingly comfortable."

His fear was that the whole situation would be too comfortable, and he wouldn't want to leave, but he knew if he wanted information from Cameron, he'd have to play by her rules. The thought plaguing him now was whether he wanted information about Red because he needed it, or he simply wanted her to tell him the story. With a phone call, he could have everything he needed to know about Red within an hour, but that only gave him an overview. What he wanted was details, so he kicked off his shoes and climbed onto the bed. He put several feet between them and laid on his back with his arms folded behind his head.

"Start at the beginning."

She flopped to her back and they both stared at the tongue-and-groove ceiling.

"I was seven pounds, six ounces when I was born."

He rolled to his side to look at her. "Not that beginning."

She laughed and faced him. "Just kidding. What do you want to know?"

The bedspread had a paisley pattern on it, and he ran his fingers around the loops and curves. He didn't know why they called it paisley when the main pattern resembled fat-tailed sperm. He knew he shouldn't have climbed into bed with her and rolled back to his back, so he didn't get distracted by her purple eyes or her rosy lips.

"Let's start with why he thinks you almost got married."

"Because he asked, and I said yes."

"Did he buy you a ring?"

The bed shook, and he figured she was gesturing but he couldn't see. "Was that a yes, or no?" He rolled over to face her again. If he could see her expressions and body movements, then this might go more quickly.

"Yes, I had a ring."

"Then he's right, you almost got married."

She lifted onto her elbow and her hair cascaded over her shoulder. "No, we got engaged. Almost getting married is walking down the aisle. It's picking out the wedding dress and the venue. We never got that far because the weekend after we got engaged, he slept with someone else."

"Idiot."

Her eyes grew wide. "Me or him?"

He shook his head. "Him."

"Why would you say that?"

"Because he didn't deserve you."

She began tracing the pattern on the spread too. "Maybe it was my fault."

"How does him cheating on you make it your fault?"

"You pointed out that I haven't lived much, so maybe I was boring or wasn't enough."

He stopped her hand mid-trace by covering it with his. "You are anything but boring. Hell, I've known you for less than a day and we've been in a plane crash, we've dined together, driven a long distance, and rented a house. I'd say you were quite exciting."

"Really?" She smiled. "It has been quite an adventure. Don't forget, we kissed."

"We did." He wished he could forget that part, but it was going to stay with him forever. The truth was, he hadn't wanted to stop kissing her in the diner, and all he could think about was kissing her again.

"In case you're curious, that kiss was almost the best part of my day."

"Almost?" He could unequivocally say that kissing her was the best part of his.

She rolled off the bed and onto her feet. "You only came in second to the wildlife and that's only because I've been kissed before, but I've never seen an elk up close and in person."

He stood and walked toward her. "Looks like I'll have to up my kissing game if I come in second to an elk."

She shrugged. "Right now, you're second. There's still Maisey's pie. You might find yourself sliding into third."

"Next time I'll hit a home run and you'll never want to kiss anyone else." The words were out before he could take them back.

"Next time, huh?"

"Shall we go taste that pie?" He needed to get their minds off kissing. He was even willing to fall to third place behind pie to do it.

"I'll race you." She tore out of the bedroom with him hot on her heels down the hallway. She flung the front door open and ran into a man. She hit him so hard, she bounced back and landed in Val's arms.

"Whoa, slow down," the man in uniform said. "I'm Sheriff

Aiden Cooper and I wanted to stop by and welcome you to Aspen Cove."

Cameron's hands went to her nose and when she dropped them, they were covered in blood. "I think your chest broke my nose."

CHAPTER THIRTEEN

Cameron raced into the bathroom to grab a wad of toilet paper. She wasn't a stranger to bloody noses. As a kid, she got plenty of them, but she hadn't had one in a long time.

"Are you okay?" Val came up behind her. "Let me see."

She shook her head. "No, I don't want you to see me." She pulled the bloody tissue away and grabbed for more but before she could get another wad, he turned her around, lifted her, and set her on the counter.

Like a medic, he went right to work cleaning her up. "It doesn't look too bad." He placed his thumbs on the sides of her nose. "I don't think it's broken, but we'll see. Aiden went to get the town doctor."

"I'm fine. I don't need a doctor." She swiped a few tissues from the box on the counter and pressed them to her nose to stop the bleeding.

"You're not fine. You're still bleeding and that had to have hurt."

Though she knew she should pinch the bridge of her nose and tilt her head back, she let her shoulders fall forward because it did hurt, and it still hurt.

"It does. Maybe your one rule should have been don't run in the house. It was a rule my mother had."

He rolled tissues into little cigars and gently placed them in her nose. "See, rules work in your favor." He thumbed her chin up and brushed the hair that had fallen in her face aside.

"Don't look at me. I look a mess."

"I don't care what you look like, but it's my job to protect you, and you're making that difficult."

She leaned forward and rested her head on his shoulder. "I don't try to be difficult. It just happens." A sob escaped and she swallowed it down.

He wrapped his arms around her and tugged her close. "It's okay. You're going to be okay."

"You seem to be telling me that a lot lately. My life was going along swimmingly until you came along."

He hugged her tightly and when he laughed, she could feel the vibration of his chest against her cheek. "You think I'm your problem?"

"I didn't have any problems until you came along." She breathed in the scent of him. Everyone had their own personal perfume. Quintin Nogono smelled like rotten eggs, but Val smelled like heaven, or maybe it was the dry-cleaning solution. All she knew was that he smelled good, and she felt good in his arms.

"You had plenty of problems before I came along but if you want to blame me for running face-first into Sheriff Cooper's chest, that's okay too."

"You're not a very good bodyguard." She leaned back and pointed to her nose. "What am I going to do if my nose is broken?" She hadn't fully thought about the implications of a broken nose. If she needed surgery, it could ruin her life. "You know, when Jennifer Grey from *Dirty Dancing* got a nose job, it ruined her career."

He lifted her from the counter and set her on her feet. "You aren't going to need a nose job, but I think an ice pack is in order. You're already turning black and blue."

"Those aren't my colors."

He took her hand and led her into the kitchen, where he pointed to a chair. "Have a seat." He looked through the cupboards and found a sandwich bag and filled it with ice. Then he located a kitchen towel and wrapped it around the ice before he walked over and pressed it to her nose. "Though I've been told that I shouldn't be a fashion consultant"—he smiled at her—"I think you'd look good in any color."

She shook her head. "Not true. I have a hard time pulling off chartreuse. It washes out my skin and makes my teeth look green." That's what her mother told her, and she'd never led her astray.

"I have no idea what color that is."

There was a soft knock at the door and Val replaced his hand on the ice pack with hers. "Hold it in place, and I'll be right back."

She sat there staring out the window. The elk were gone, and the sun was almost set. Only a sliver of orange showed against an almost purple sky.

In walked Val and two men.

The sheriff walked over first, probably because he was younger and faster. The older man seemed to shuffle along. She was quite surprised that he did house calls.

"I'm sorry my chest got in your way."

She wanted to laugh but knew it would hurt. "I'm sorry for trying to plow you over, but in all fairness, there was pie involved."

"Maisey's pie?" the sheriff asked.

She nodded and regretted the move. "Berry pie."

The sheriff smiled and nodded. "It's worth the two black eyes you're going to get."

"Move out of my way," the doctor said. "All this chitchat is eating up my Dancing with the Stars time. Lovey made rice crispy treats and I don't want to miss the finale."

"Can I speak to you, Sheriff?" Val asked, and the two men moved into the living room, leaving her alone with the crotchety old doctor. He reminded her of one of the docs they had on set once when she got tonsillitis. On the outside, he was meaner than a junkyard dog, but on the inside, he was a marshmallow, all soft and sweet, and she wondered if this man was the same.

"Now who do we have here?"

"I'm Cameron." Her voice sounded muffled but that was because she had the equivalent of two tampons shoved up her nose and an ice pack to help with the suffocation.

"Yep, I know who you are. I've seen quite a few of your movies. My Lovey is a fan of your Christmas shows. I think she liked Red Bows and Raymond the best. It's like a classic for her." He pulled the ice pack off and let out a whistle. "That was some hit." He felt her nose, running his finger along the bridge and sides. "You're lucky. It's not broken, but it's bruised badly."

"How bad does it look?"

He got closer and then stood back. "I've seen worse."

That didn't fill her with confidence.

"Will it heal on its own?" Val asked as he walked back into the kitchen.

Doc took out the tissue inside her nose. "She's one tough cookie." He turned back to look at the sheriff. "Hitting him is like hitting a block wall."

Cameron gently touched her nose. "Tell me about it."

"Take two ibuprofen every four to six hours as needed for

discomfort. Keep ice on it for swelling—twenty minutes every hour or two until the swelling subsides. Keep your head elevated when you're sleeping and don't call me during the finale." He picked up his black bag from the table and stared at the sheriff. "I'm ready to go."

"It's nice to meet you, Doctor Parker."

He waved his hand through the air. "Wait until you get my bill." He chuckled as he shuffled toward the door. "Everyone calls me Doc. Since you're here, you're part of everyone."

"Thank you, Doc." Val pulled out his wallet which seemed to have an endless supply of money. "How much do I owe you?"

Doc laughed. "You can pay up someday at Bishop's Brewhouse. I'm there at four every day. Don't be late if it's Thursday because I have to be out of there by five. It's pot roast night at the diner, and I don't want to miss it." He got to the front door and said out loud, "Lovey, I'm coming. Don't eat the last rice crispy treat."

The sheriff shook Val's hand and turned to her. "It's a pleasure meeting you, Ms. Madden. My wife and daughter are fans."

Cameron smiled. "Let me know where I can find them, and I'll stop by and say hello."

The sheriff's eyes grew wide. "That would be mighty nice of you." He walked toward the door and stopped. "You don't need to worry about anyone in town. They all know you're here by now, but no one will bother you. We take pride in being the type of town whose residents are here when you need them and absent when you don't." He glanced at Val. "Red won't be a problem. I'll make sure of it."

He turned and walked away, leaving her and Val alone.

"Can I get you anything?" Val asked.

She nodded. "I still want my pie."

He raced out the door and came back with the to-go containers and their bags of clothes. "How about we enjoy dessert on the deck?"

"Do you think it's safe to go out there?" she teased.

"Probably not. With your luck, an owl with a poor navigation system will swoop down and beak you in the head. I'm starting to think that you're the unlucky one in our group of two."

She rose and headed for the deck. "You're probably right." She picked up a bottle of wine from the rack and the opener she found nearby. "Can you bring two glasses while you're getting the pie? I'll try not to poke an eye out with the opener."

He stared at her like she was serious. "Better not take any chances." He took the bottle, opened it, and poured two glasses. "Do you think you can get these to the deck safely or should I get you settled and come back for them?"

"I'll be fine." She took the glass and started for the door. As a joke, she kicked the bottom of the door jamb and let out a screech and a groan and waited. It took Val a few seconds to come to her rescue, but by then she was leaning on the handrail sipping her wine.

"What the hell was that? I thought you fell or something."

She winked. "That was good acting."

He set the two pie plates on the table that was between two Adirondack chairs and took the glass of wine she offered. "Here's to your Oscar-worthy performance, but if you do that again, I'll turn you over my knee."

She laughed. "I might like that." She couldn't believe she said that and quickly took a seat, set her wine down, and shoved a bite of pie into her mouth so she didn't say anything else.

Val leaned against the rail and stared at her. She tried to read his expression and what she saw was part agitation and a dark look of desire. Or maybe she had a head injury because it sure felt like her nose got shoved into her brain.

"Are you going to eat your pie?"

He pushed away from the rail and took a seat. "Why, do you want it?"

"Are you kidding? I've eaten a year's worth of carbs since I met you. You are not good for me."

He sipped his wine and stared at the lake. "That's the most accurate thing you've said all day."

He was probably right but being with Val made her feel alive for the first time. Why did she always choose the wrong men?

CHAPTER FOURTEEN

He sipped his wine and stared out at the lake. This was his vision of heaven. All he needed to make it perfect was a fishing pole and a rowboat.

"Why do you hate what you do?" Cameron asked.

"I don't." It wasn't a lie; he didn't hate it, but he didn't choose it. He was good at it, but his father had taught him that no matter what he did, he had to give his all, and he'd been doing that since he could remember. "It's busy. I'm never anywhere for long. I live out of a carry-on bag."

"You said that if you weren't doing this, then you'd be running an outdoor adventure company. Tell me what that would look like."

He kicked his legs out and crossed them at the ankles. "I've never thought about what it would look like because it's not an option."

She turned in her chair and brought her knees up to her chest. "Why isn't it?"

"For the same reasons leaving acting is not an option for you. You don't act because you chose it, you do it because you don't know any better. You're an extension of your mother."

"I wish. If that were true, I'd have a bookshelf full of awards."

"That's right, you want the names."

She stared at him for a moment. "All actors want an Oscar, Emmy, or Golden Globe. It means something."

"I get that it means something to others, but what does it mean to you?" He was curious if she even realized she was living in her mother's shadow. She entered a career not because she wanted it but because Beverly wanted it for her. Thinking that made his head explode because he'd done the same. There was never a conversation about what he wanted; he was born and raised to run Vortex Security Services and when his father died, he was forever tied to it.

"It means that I was good enough."

He thought about her words. Some people needed others to validate them. He was never like that. He had a strong self-assurance gene. In his business, he had to be confident. A lack of it could result in disaster

"You were born good enough."

"I wish that were true. I work really hard. Yes, my mother was incredibly famous, and I've lived in her shadow all my life."

He was glad she had enough self-awareness to realize that. "Go on."

"It isn't easy being the child of a famous star. Everything I get, people think it's because of her and not because I earned it."

"What do you think?" That was the real question. Did she think she earned her success or was it given to her?

"I worked my ass off. While other kids were out being kids, I studied scripts, took dance and acting classes. While my friends were traveling through Europe in the summer, I was on set working."

"You have friends?"

She rocked her head back and forth. "It's a loose term. My best friend was always my mom."

"And your dad?"

"Who knows? I've asked several times, but I think my mother truly believes she was artificially inseminated by an angel one night."

"Have you ever point-blank asked her?"

She nodded. "Yes, and that's pretty much what I get. I always thought my father was Lucifer, but it isn't."

"Thank God, there are enough horror flicks about that."

She laughed. "That's Lucky's real name."

He smiled. "I know."

"Of course, you do. Was that homework for you too?"

"I'm very thorough. It's important to know who you're working for."

"What about you?"

He turned to look at her and the moonlight reflected off her eyes, making them the deepest purple without turning black.

"I know who mine is." He sipped his wine. "I'll tell you what. Let's call your mother and demand an answer. Part of you coming here was to find yourself and knowing where you came from is important. Besides, she'll be waiting to hear from you."

She pulled her lip between her teeth and gnawed on it for a second. "I'll make you a deal. I'll call my mother, but you have to do something out of your comfort zone too."

"Are we back to negotiating? I don't need to know critical information about my past. My life is perfectly fine."

She rolled her eyes. "Your life is boring. I mean, I thought mine was bad, but you..."

"What's wrong with me?"

She stared at him. "Do you want a list?"

"Do I need one?"

"Probably, because you're strung tighter than a cello string, and I know how tight those are because I took lessons when my mom heard about an upcoming movie about a savant cellist."

"I'm not strung tight. I have a serious job and I can't let my guard down or someone gets hurt or worse."

She sat up and gripped her glass of wine. "You know what you are?"

"I bet you're going to tell me."

"You're a fun sucker."

"A what?"

She emptied her glass and set it on the table. "You don't even know what that is which is sad in itself."

"I have fun."

Her eyes got big and questioning. "Oh yeah? Tell me, when was the last time you had fun?"

He knew exactly when that was; a couple hours ago, at the diner, when he kissed her. That was a whole hell of a lot of fun, but he wouldn't tell her that. "It was fun watching you climb down from the ambulance, swipe your hair back, and tell people you were auditioning for a part."

"I'm not talking about making fun of people. I'm asking you when the last time was that you actually let your rules go and had fun for fun's sake."

He sat there and stared at the lake trying to remember when he'd last had a good time.

"See, you can't even recall one time."

"Not true, I had an amazing time hiking the Grand Canyon after my high school graduation."

She looked at him with disbelief. "You enjoyed it, but was there a moment when you had a belly laugh or did

107

something silly enough to someday tell your grandchildren?"

She had him there. It was a solitary hike, but it was a wonderful experience because no one had any expectations. It was just him and the earth co-existing as one.

"Okay, you're right. I'm not a fun guy."

She moved her finger back and forth. "Not true. You have potential. I saw it when you wore those silly banana pants and asked me if your shoes matched. Somewhere deep down inside you is a fun-lover waiting to escape. So, if you want me to call my mother, then you have to get out of your comfort zone and drop your rules. We made a pact on the plane that we'd live our lives the way we wanted if we made it out of there. Look at how easily we slid back into our norm."

She was right. "We're only doing what we do."

She pointed to her nose which didn't look as bad as he thought it would. She'd have black eyes, but it wouldn't take away from her beauty. "This isn't my normal life."

He chuckled. "You wanted to find out who you are, right? Well, let me tell you, I've never met a woman with more courage and strength." He shook his head. "That's not true, there's my mother and sister. They're up there too."

"Really?" She sat up like his words lifted her.

"I mean it. I wouldn't have expected someone like you to take the punches so well. You're tough as hell."

"Why, thank you." She tapped her chin. "And your kisses were better than the elk."

He tried to contain his smile, but he couldn't. "I appreciate the vote of confidence."

"You're welcome. Now if you'll hand me your phone, I'll call my mother and get some answers."

"Perfect, and while you're talking to her, I'll set up your phone." He handed over his phone and walked inside the house to get her phone and the bottle of wine. When he came back out, she was talking and hit the speaker button so he could hear.

"I need to know, Mom."

"It's not Lucky."

She growled. "I get that, but then who?" She pressed the speaker button then brought her fingers to her lips.

"Fine, it was Clark Gable."

Cameron took in a big breath and sighed. "He died before you were born."

"Which makes him the perfect candidate for your heavenly conception." Her mother giggled. "Honey, why the desperate need to know now?"

"Because I have a right to know where I came from. I want to know who gave me these purple eyes. I want to know why my hair is blonde, and why I'm five foot two and not taller like you. I'm on a self-discovery journey, and I need you to stop joking with me. It's not that I didn't think you were enough because you were, it's just that I need more." Her eyes grew wide as if she'd just realized something. "I can't figure out who I am if I don't know who I am."

There was a moment of silence and then her mother let out an audible exhale. "I wanted you so much, that I would have done anything to have you, and I did. I went to a sperm bank."

Cameron's mouth dropped open. "Why wouldn't you tell me that?"

"Because no kid wants to know they're the offspring of donor #381."

"My father is #381?"

"I don't know his number, but that's just what came to my head. Look, I didn't want to be like so many actresses and spend my best years giving myself to Hollywood, and then when it chewed me up and spit me out, what would be left? I wanted it all, and I took all life would allow me. I had a wonderful career, and I had you."

"But what about love?"

"That's something that wasn't meant to be. What about you, honey? What do you want?"

Val poured the wine and stared at Cameron as she contemplated her mother's question. "I want it all too."

"Then go after what you want. If you can dream it, you can have it. I've always told you that."

Cameron nodded. "You did." She picked up her full glass of wine and took a big swig. "Mom?"

"Yes, honey?"

"You were always enough."

"I love you, sweetheart. Follow your heart when your head is confused. It will never lead you astray."

Cameron and her mother said their goodbyes and hung up. He activated her phone and handed it to her. "Are you okay?"

The water lapped at the shore in the distance. The white bubbles caught the light of the moon, making the shore look like it was made from cut lace.

"I am. I would have been angrier if she said it was Lucky, and they'd kept it from me all these years. She hid the truth to protect me. People who love you protect you."

They did, and that was why he'd stayed as the head of Vortex all these years. He loved his family and he thought he was protecting them but was he? Listening to Cameron and Beverly's conversation made him think about his own life. What Beverly did was both admirable and despicable. She hadn't considered what the lack of information would do to her daughter. It made him wonder if keeping Vortex, the way his father had wanted, meant that his brothers and sister never fully realized who they were either. Had they all been living a lie to please each other? It was something he'd have to think about another day. Right now, he had a debt to pay. She'd done as he asked and so he owed her a fun-lover moment.

"What did you have in mind for fun?" He glanced at her when she didn't answer and found she'd fallen asleep. He chuckled and rose from his seat. "You're a bundle of fun tonight, I see." He scooped her up and she wrapped her arms around his neck, laying her head on his chest. "Let's get you to bed. We can start the fun tomorrow." He walked her into her room and placed her on the bed. She turned to her side and pulled the bedspread over her.

He reached under and took off her shoes before he tucked the blanket under her chin and kissed her on the cheek. "You're the most fun I've had in my lifetime." He walked out and went to his room wondering what the hell was he going to do about his feelings for Cameron Madden?

CHAPTER FIFTEEN

Cameron woke early. She'd never excelled at sleeping, but that was more of her mother's habit than hers. All her life her mother drilled in the importance of seizing the day, and if there was daylight, there was opportunity.

She tossed off the covers and realized she was dressed in yesterday's clothes. "How did I get to bed?" She'd only had a couple glasses of wine, but she imagined the last few days' events had caught up to her. Her last memory was talking to Val on the deck and then nothing.

She rocked to her feet and headed to the bathroom where she gasped at her reflection. Her nose seemed to look mostly normal except for a little swelling, but her eyes were both black and blue. She'd need to put her best makeup artist skills to the test after her shower.

When she came out, she felt like an entirely new person. She'd done the best job she could to camouflage the bruising, but it still showed, especially where the bridge of her nose met the corners of her eyes. Nothing was taking that eggplant color away.

She found her clothes hanging in the closet and imagined

Val had brought them in and hung them up. For a grumpy man, he knew how to spread sunshine at just the right moments.

She picked out a pair of jeans and a white eyelet blouse with puffy sleeves. It wasn't something she'd ever wear in Hollywood, but it made her inner child happy to put it on. Who knew dressing down could bring such joy. At the thought of joy, she recalled their conversation last night. She'd done what he'd asked and confronted her mom which meant he owed her a moment of fun, and no day could be fun without coffee, and the perfect thing to go with coffee was a muffin. Since Val had started her day off perfectly with access to her clothes, she thought she'd return the favor.

On a normal day, she'd head to the gym in the building and run on the treadmill, but this was a different life and with it came different opportunities.

She tiptoed down the hallway to Val's room, where she peeked in and found him fast asleep. Then she snuck into the kitchen to get her bag and slipped out the front door. The air was crisp and cool at seven in the morning. In the trees above, birds chirped as if they were taking roll call to find out who made it through the night. Two squirrels were having an argument of some kind until one raced past her and up a tree.

Her life didn't allow her to spend much time alone. There was always someone with her, whether it was security or cast and crew. She knew Val wouldn't be happy that she ventured out by herself, but she needed to see the world through her own eyes for a change. If he was walking with her, she'd see it through his paranoia. Thinking about that made her heart race.

She glanced behind her to make sure she wasn't being followed. When the coast was clear, her nerves settled, and she continued down Lake Circle until she needed to make a right turn onto Main Street.

The town was small, but it was quaint. Along her path, she passed by houses of every architectural style. To her left was an elaborate Victorian decked out in yellow, pink, and green paint. On her right was a cabin that sat next to a bungalow that set next to a home that looked older, but also seemed brand new. The yards were planted with flowers ranging from daisies to roses to hydrangeas. Hydrangeas were her favorite flowers. The big white, pink, and green pompoms brought a smile to her face every time she saw them.

As she entered town she passed by the sheriff's station. The lights were off, and no one was there. Did crime happen on a schedule in Aspen Cove? She giggled to herself because she couldn't imagine crime happening in a place where everyone had to know each other.

Next door was Bishop's Brewhouse and it also seemed abandoned. She peeked in the windows and saw the bar, with its chairs stacked on the tables and a floor that looked clean enough to eat off. Movement caught her attention, and she zoned in on a cat who sat on a table basking in the first ray of sunshine. She closed her eyes and lifted her nose into the air. The smell of chocolate and sweetness swirled around her and pulled her farther down the street past Bishop's Bait and Tackle Shop to B's Bakery. The lights were on and inside was a woman rushing around like her bottom was on fire.

Cameron tried the door and to her surprise, it opened. The bell attached sounded with a pleasant jingle and the woman behind the counter said, "Aiden, I'm running a bit behind today." She popped up and smiled. "Oh, I'm sorry. I thought you were Sheriff Cooper." The woman stared at her like she was taking a test and Cameron was the last question. "Do I know you?"

Cameron shook her head. "No." She might have seen her on television but that didn't mean the woman knew her.

"Let me make you a cup of coffee. Everything should be ready in a few minutes." The pretty blonde woman walked to the coffee machine and popped in a plastic cup and pressed start. "Sage is still on me about getting one of those fancy espresso machines, but honestly, most people love my Keurig."

Cameron loved the southern lilt to the woman's voice. "You're not from here, are you?"

The coffee finished brewing and the woman put her cup on the counter and offered her hand. "Forgive my bad manners. I'm Katie Bishop."

Cameron took her hand and shook it. "I'm Cameron Madden."

A knowing look washed over Katie. "Oh, I know who you are." She leaned in and smiled. "I just loved you in Royally Stacked."

"Thank you." That had been one of Cameron's favorites too because what woman doesn't want to be a princess? In that movie, she played a librarian who met a prince hiding from his family. It was charming and sweet and full of swoon-worthy moments and her costar didn't stink.

She took a sip of the coffee and sighed. "This is good. I wouldn't change a thing." Then she remembered that she didn't have any money. "Oh, my goodness. I need an ATM. I have no money." The color must have left her face because Katie looked concerned.

"Don't worry. I'm not going to call the sheriff if you can't pay. Besides, the first coffee and muffin are on the house." She pointed to a table that sat under a bulletin board labeled The Wishing Wall. "Have a seat, and I'll join you. Today is raspberry muffin day which means the sheriff should be around soon."

Cameron took a seat. "The lights were off at the sheriff's office when I passed."

Katie smiled. "Aiden must be helping Marina with the kids then."

Cameron loved how sweet that sounded. "I ran into him last night." She ghosted her finger across her nose which was sensitive to the lightest touch. "Literally."

Katie came around the counter and took the seat on the other side of the table. "I was wondering what happened to you, but I'd never ask." She pointed to her eyes. "But now that you brought it up, it's open season. What happened?"

"Exactly what I said. I was running out the door to get Maisey's pie from the car, and I ran straight into his chest which felt like hitting a wall."

When a buzzer went off, Katie stood. "Don't go anywhere." She rushed around the counter and opened the oven.

While she was busy, Cameron looked at the board above her. "What's this wall about?"

"It's exactly what it says. Give it a try. Take a sticky note and write what you want on it. I've found that putting it to paper makes it real and not just a dream. Then once it's down, you get to give it to the universe to work on."

"So, it's like a manifestation board?"

She placed a box on the counter and put a tray of muffins in the display case. A moment later she came back to the table with a plate of muffins.

"I guess so, but it's more like the *Wizard of Oz*, and I'm the guy behind the curtain. I try to grant all the wishes that I can and those I can't I leave up to the universe."

"That's amazing."

Katie pulled off a sticky note and handed her a pen. "Try it. Write down what you want."

Cameron stared at the note and pen. "It kind of feels selfish to ask for something when I have so much."

Katie laughed. "Obviously, you're not from the 'there's never enough' group." She waved her hand in the air. "Just fill it out. What can it hurt?"

The bell above the door rang and in walked Sheriff Cooper. He saw her at the table and rushed over. "How's the nose?"

"I survived."

He shook his head. "You're one tough cookie." He looked around. "Where's Val?"

"I left him in bed asleep." As soon as the words were out, she knew how they sounded so she clarified. "*His* bed. We aren't, you know ... a thing." That felt like a lie inside because she liked him and could see him being someone who would be a good thing in her life, but like most of the people around, he was hired.

"And he knows that you're here alone?" The sheriff narrowed his eyes before he rubbed at the jaw of his clean-shaven face.

"Umm, no. Remember, he's asleep."

Aiden swiped the box of muffins from the counter and walked toward the door. "I can't wait to see how that goes over."

Katie pushed the note forward. "I can't do anything about your security person's personality."

Cameron thought about what she wished for most in life, and that was to get the role of a lifetime, so she wrote it down. "I fear you can't help me here either, but it doesn't hurt to put it to paper." She stood and pressed it to the board. When it fell off, Katie handed her a thumbtack. "Give it a good poke. I find sometimes mother nature needs a needle in the ass to get her moving." She pointed to the muffin. "Take a bite and tell me if you like it. If you don't, just lie because my most recent wish is to make muffins that everyone likes."

Cameron liked Katie; she was sweet and easy to talk to. She took a bite of the warm muffin and didn't have to question why they were the sheriff's favorite. "So good."

Katie beamed. "What do you mean by the role of a lifetime?"

Cameron thought about her wish and realized it was vague. She reached for it, but Katie shook her head. "It's already up there so you can't take it down."

"I want a role that defines me."

Katie sat back and by her thoughtful expression, it was easy to see she was thinking that over. "Why wouldn't you want to define yourself?"

For the next twenty minutes, Katie told Cameron her story. "So, you see, I know what it's like to not fully realize my true potential. While I'd like to blame everyone around me, I had a responsibility to define myself, to set my own standards and demand more for myself, and when I did..." She spread her arms and looked around the bakery. "My life began."

"Your life would make an amazing movie."

Katie laughed. "Do you want to play me?"

"It would be my honor."

She pointed to the note. "Well, that could be your role of a lifetime but somehow my intuition tells me it's not a part you're looking for."

She shook her head. "No, you're wrong. It is a part."

"Hmmm, are you sure? Be careful what you ask for, you might actually get it." The buzzer went off and Katie went behind the counter to open the oven. The smell of chocolate wafted through the space. "You have to taste one of these brownies."

"How are you not fat?"

Katie laughed. "I have a toddler. Well, she's really three going on thirty, but she keeps me busy."

The door opened and all the feeling of rainbows and unicorns left when she watched Red walk inside.

He noticed her right away and rushed over. "What the hell happened to you?"

"That's not very nice."

"If that son of a—"

The door opened and a shadow fell over her. "Get away from her." Val's voice took on a sinister tone. "You've got about three seconds to act on your own, or I'll remove you myself."

Red stood in front of her. "I'm not going anywhere. Did you give her that black eye?"

Cameron stood and shoved Red out of the way. "Of course not. Sheriff Cooper gave it to me." Cameron walked to the counter. "Can I get another coffee and muffin to go?" She moved over to Val. "I need to borrow some money. I forgot I didn't have any."

Red opened his wallet and took out a twenty. "Here you go." He turned to Val. "I've got it."

Val stepped forward. "Leave. Now."

"You can't make me leave. It's a public place."

Val smiled and looked at Katie. "Ma'am, can you call the sheriff, and tell him he's needed." He looked at Red. "You might want to get the doc too because if this man doesn't step away from Cameron, he'll need medical care in a few seconds."

Cameron knew she shouldn't have been turned on by that, but she'd never experienced anything like it. While Val was simply doing his job, she liked the way his possessiveness felt. It was like he truly cared.

Katie set a muffin and coffee on the counter and then picked up the phone.

"It's okay, Katie, we're leaving. Mr. Grumpy just needs coffee and something sweet." She looked up at Val. "Pay the girl and let's go."

He stood there for a second before he took money from his wallet and set it on the counter.

"First visit is free," Katie said.

"It's a tip," Val growled.

Cameron handed him the coffee and muffin, then turned and looked at Red. "Here's a tip for you. Don't mess with my boyfriend. He loves me like you never could." She tucked her arm through his and walked to the front door. "You ready to go, love?"

Outside he led her away and stopped in front of the bait and tackle store. "You broke a rule. You left without my permission."

She rolled her eyes. "You promised me you'd have fun and look at you. You're back to being a fun sucker."

"You left and I didn't know where you were."

"Where could I be? Look around you. There's nothing here."

The door opened to the bakery and out walked Red. His face reflected his name.

Val nodded toward him. "He's here, and he's a problem."

"For who? If I didn't know better, I'd say you were jealous."

His head snapped back like she'd slapped him. "He's a threat."

"Not to me. He's an asshole. Now drink your coffee and eat something. You're acting like you're hangry. That happens to me sometimes."

"I'm not hangry, but I'm not happy."

She laughed. "That's good to know because if this is you being happy, we need to renegotiate my prize for confronting my mom. What will make you happy?"

He looked over his shoulder. "I want to go camping."

Camping sounded like a nightmare to her but if it made him happy then she'd do it.

The closed sign on the bait and tackle store flipped over and the man behind the door unlocked it. She took Val's hand and pulled him to the door. "I bet he can help."

CHAPTER SIXTEEN

Before he could stop her, Cameron opened the door and walked inside. He had no other choice but to follow her since she was dragging him by the hand.

"Welcome to Bishop's, can I help you?" The guy who opened the door took his place behind the counter and nodded. He wasn't the smiling type of guy. Val understood his type. He'd taken all the personality tests and profiles and his always identified him as being serious, or, as Cameron would say, a fun sucker.

"We're just looking."

She shook her head. "That's a lie. Please forgive him. He hasn't eaten this morning." She took the muffin, which he was balancing on the top of his cup, pulled off a chunk and pressed it against his lips. "Eat before we really have to call the sheriff." She turned and smiled at the guy staring at them. "I'm ready to commit murder, so hide all the weapons." She glanced around the shop which was mostly fishing gear and pointed to the large stuffed fish on the wall. "Not that, because if you have to die, you might as well go out on a fantastical note, and being bludgeoned by a grouper is newsworthy."

"It's a bass," the guy said. "It was eight pounds when it was alive." He stared at Val. "Do you like the muffins? My wife made them."

"Just say yes. She's got a goal to make a muffin that everyone loves."

"I don't have to lie, it's the best muffin ever."

"Good to hear. I'm Bowie and I'm glad I didn't have to use that bass to defend my Katie's baking."

Cameron walked over and shook the man's hand. "Your wife is my favorite person in town." She glanced over her shoulder. "It would be him if he knew what fun looked like, which is why we're here. He wants to go camping."

"We're a bait and tackle shop."

"I know, but surely because it's outdoor stuff, it's similar, right?"

Bowie cocked his head and stared at Val. "Do you want to explain it to her?"

Val shook his head. "No, man, this is your lane. You go right ahead."

"Comparing fishing to camping is like…" He paused for a moment and Val knew he was trying to figure out how to compare things that Cameron would understand. She might look as country as can be in her jeans and flouncy shirt, but she had an air about her that screamed money. "It's like saying Motel 6 and the Ritz are the same. They're both hotels but you can't really compare the two. Fishing and camping happen outside but they aren't really the same. Now, you can fish while you're camping, but that's all about the location."

Cameron held her hand up. She reached for his coffee and muffin and set them on the table. "We'll be right back." She took Val's hand and marched him back to the bakery where she took a pen and sticky note from the wall. "Write it down."

"Write what down?"

Katie leaned on the counter watching him. "Your wish. You write it down and it comes true ... sometimes."

"This is ridiculous."

"I'm not having fun," Cameron said, and she stomped a foot and frowned.

He took the paper and pen and wrote *I wish I could go camping.* He showed it to her. "Fine, are you happy?"

Cameron shook her head. "Not until you are."

She took the note and thumbtacked it to the board. "Katie, this needs to happen now. Please call your husband. He looks like a resourceful man."

Katie raced around the counter and swiped the note from the board.

"Hey," Val said. "That's my wish."

Cameron took his hand and tugged him toward the door. "Don't worry, she's Oz."

He had no idea what she was talking about, but he followed her out the door and back to the bait and tackle shop. When they walked inside, Bowie was on the phone. "Yes, love. I'm on it." He hung up and smiled. "I hear you want to go camping."

"That's right and we need everything," Cameron said.

"Do you know where you want to go?"

Val went to open his mouth, but Cameron stepped in. "Nope, just send us somewhere beautiful and relaxing."

Bowie nodded. "Okay, give me a few hours and I'll figure something out."

Cameron ran behind the counter and threw her arms around Bowie. "Thank you."

The man sat there stiffly while she hugged him, and it wasn't until she pulled away that he relaxed.

"How many days?"

Cameron lifted her shoulders. "That's up to him."

If it was truly up to him, they'd backpack into the mountains until the first snow fell, but it wasn't up to him. "A few days." He nodded to Cameron. "I don't think she can handle more than that. After sleeping in the wild, she'll think Motel 6 is the Ritz."

"Ha ha, don't forget, I'm made of tough stuff. I survived a plane crash, and a seven-hour drive with you."

He couldn't take that away from her. Not the drive because that was easy, but she was made of tough stuff, and he admired her for that.

"He'd like to fish too. Cost is not an issue. I'd pay anything to see him have a second of fun."

"Hey, I have fun," Val said.

She huffed. "Threatening Red Blakely to within an inch of his life was entertaining but I wouldn't call it fun."

Bowie raised his hand. "You're wrong there. That would be fun."

After talking to the sheriff, Val knew that Red wasn't a beloved member of the community. When he said the man was trouble, he knew what he was talking about. Red might have been a cheater, but when he saw Cameron again, he was more like a dog and Cameron was the bone. Red was the type of guy who fished with a net and looked through the catch and tossed aside what he didn't want until someone else wanted it. Now that he thought Cameron was with Val, Red was twice as interested in what he had tossed aside.

"Let me see what I can do. Are you staying at Frank's place?"

"How did you know?" Cameron asked.

Bowie tapped his head. "I'm the town psychic." Then he laughed. "Not really. My brother is Cannon, who owns the bar, and his wife owns the only bed and breakfast in town. His place is filled with a bunch of fishermen this week and since you two don't have any equipment, I deduced that you aren't staying there. Frank recently started renting his place out. Rumor had it that someone famous was coming to town." He looked at Val. "I didn't know it would be Jason Statham with hair."

"See," Cameron said. "Even he had fun. It's at your expense, but it was funny. Don't shoot him, okay?"

Bowie's eyes grew wide, and Val went to Cameron and wrapped his arm around her shoulders. "No one is getting shot today." He turned and looked at her. "Grounded, yes, but shot ... no." He walked her to the door. "You know where to find us if you can help pull it off. We need everything and can settle the bill later."

Bowie chuckled. "Dude, did you meet my wife at the bakery? I don't have a choice but to pull it off. I'd say be ready to leave in the morning."

As they walked outside, he turned to Cameron. "You're in trouble, but I really am hungry, and I never punish anyone on an empty stomach."

"Punish me?" By the look on her face, she wasn't sure if he was serious or not and he liked that she was uncertain.

"Don't ever leave the house without me."

"I was getting you breakfast. You did so many kind things like put me into bed and hang up my clothes. I wanted to do something nice for you."

How could he be mad at her for that? He shouldn't have been, but he was. "Next time you want to do something kind for me, let me know."

"But the surprise was half of the gift."

"Oh, it was a surprise all right to get up and find you gone. I only knew where you were because I had to have Viv hack into the phone system and put a tracker on your phone. Now my family thinks I'm incompetent."

"You? Incompetent? Hardly." They walked across the street and into the diner. "Look, I peeked in on you and you were asleep. You looked so peaceful."

Now he knew he was off his game. He had slept like a bear in the winter. That wasn't like him. "I need one rule. If you don't give me anything else, I need this."

He looked around the almost-full diner and found an empty table in the center. It wasn't ideal but it was all they had. He pulled out a chair for Cameron and sat across from her.

"There you go with your rules again."

"I'm only asking for one thing."

She rubbed her temples. "If I remember correctly, you only had one rule before, and it was that you made all the rules. Is that what you're going to say this time too?"

"No."

She heaved in a heavy breath. "Fine, I'll give you one. What is it?" She gripped the butter knife. "But if you say it's that you make all the rules, I'll stab you and tell everyone I'm practicing for a part."

"I need to know you're safe and the only way that can happen is if you're always with me. Do not leave without letting me know." He wanted to say without his permission, but he knew that wouldn't go over well.

"Fine." She looked over her shoulder. "Can I use the restroom?"

"You don't have to ask my permission." He was glad that she did though because it meant she understood what he really needed.

She slid her chair back and stood. "When Maisey comes back, I'd like hot cocoa and pancakes, please."

Maisey sauntered over with her coffee pot. "Back so soon?"

He turned over the mug on the table. "Cameron is on a mission to leave no carb behind."

Maisey smiled. "I love a girl who can eat."

"So do I." That was another thing that he liked about her. She was a movie star and here she was in public sporting two black eyes, poorly covered by makeup, and she was going to shove her face full of pancakes and hot cocoa. He placed their order and Maisey left to fill it.

When Cameron got back to the table, she leaned in and said, "Why did you let me leave the house looking so awful?" A second later she smiled. "Just kidding, but seriously, I look like I lost a fight."

"Keep telling people you're researching for a part."

She smiled and his heart flipped and flopped. "It seems to be my go-to line when I'm with you. But I do look dreadful."

He reached across and patted her hand. "You look like a winner." In his opinion, she did. She was like a Timex watch. Years ago, they had a campaign that said, "Takes a lickin' and keeps on tickin'." Yep, Cameron Madden was made of tough stuff.

CHAPTER SEVENTEEN

After breakfast, they took the car back to the house and waited for Bowie to contact them. As she sat on the deck watching the lake, energy surged through her veins. It was rather exciting to have an upcoming trip that was a surprise to both. For her, it was so out of the norm because her life was planned down to the time she got anywhere, to the time allotted to pee. She imagined the entire event was making Val apoplectic. He was the planner—the guy who had everything from the stop lights to the bus schedules coordinated perfectly to ensure nothing went sideways.

"Are you excited?"

He frowned but nodded. "The idea is intriguing, but the prospect of someone else planning it makes me itch. How can I protect you if I don't have all the details?"

"Let's pretend you don't have to protect me."

He rubbed his knuckles against his eyes. "That's the whole reason I'm here. If you didn't need protection, then hiring me was a waste of your resources."

She shrugged. "They're my resources, so you don't have to worry about it." She hated that in her life it was all about the money. People were so hyper-focused on the money that they often overlooked everything else.

"Does your company do well?" She imagined it had to. They didn't advertise. All their business was done by word of mouth.

"We do okay."

That wasn't really what she was after. She didn't want to see his profit and loss statements, but she needed to know if this job made a difference to his bottom line.

"I'm sure you do. You come highly recommended." She fidgeted with her hair and turned to face him. He was dressed in a pair of jeans and a T-shirt that hugged him like a possessive lover. Val was a handsome man. He fell right in line with the kind of guy she was attracted to. He was tall and put together but had that bad-boy air that she found so exciting. "Have you ever killed anyone?" She was getting off track, but she wanted to know. It was simply a morbid curiosity.

He leaned back in the Adirondack chair. "You want to know if I've killed anyone?"

"I understand it's part of your job and maybe your non-disclosure agreement with your clients prevents you from divulging the details, but I am curious."

"I operate my business within the confines of the law and killing people is illegal. Having said that, if I was protecting a client and had to shoot someone in that capacity, I'd aim to injure, not to kill."

He was skating all around the question. "Just answer the damn question."

"No, I haven't had to shoot anyone, but I've wanted to." He rubbed his shoulder. "I even asked Carlo if I could shoot his son to teach him a lesson about firing a weapon, but he let Isabella beat that lesson into him with her cast iron skillet."

She watched as he rubbed his shoulder. "Does it pain you much?"

He grabbed the hem of his cotton shirt and pulled it over his head. He pointed to his left shoulder where there was a divot the size of a baby carrot.

"Ow, wow." She rose from her chair and went to him, then gingerly touched the scar. It was healed but red and angry looking. As she skirted her fingertips over the rough surface, goosebumps rose on his skin, and she wondered if it was from the chill in the air or her touch.

"Is this the first time you've been shot?"

He shook his head. "No Vivian shot me in the thigh once."

"Your sister shot you?"

He chuckled. "It was an accident. I was teaching her gun safety."

"Obviously she failed that class." She laid her hands on his back and kneaded the tight muscles.

He groaned and leaned back into her touch. "She'll never make that mistake again." He shifted his body, so her hands were exactly where he wanted them. "Where did you learn to do that?" He relaxed and then stiffened. "And please don't tell me you did it to relax Red after a concert."

She kept at the tight muscles until they turned soft under her fingers. "No, I learned this for a movie where I played a masseuse."

He cocked his head. "That one where you played opposite the banker?"

A giddy feeling raced up her spine. "You really did watch all my movies."

"I never lie."

She liked that about him. The problem with most people was that they lied all the time. It was an issue for her because people never gave her the down-and-dirty truth. They sugar-coated things so as not to offend. Don't burn bridges was the law in Hollywood. The guy who was the extra today in a film might very well be the leading man in the next. And for women ... well, it was an altogether different experience. She'd been lucky to have Lucky. He protected her from the Harvey Weinsteins and the casting couches that seemed to plague many a starlet.

"I try hard to make sure the parts I play are portrayed real-istically. I've taken classes on massage. I worked in a library to make my part realistic. I even waited on people at a diner for a few weeks." She giggled. "I wore a fake mole on my lip and a red wig, so no one recognized me."

"Did that work?"

"It did until the mole fell into some guy's chicken soup and when I bent over to scoop it up my wig fell in his lap."

She patted his shoulders and walked around to take her chair. Sadly, Val pulled his shirt back on and the view was less invigorating than it had been moments before. Even the lake looked more beautiful when he was bare-chested.

The doorbell rang and Val rose. "I'd tell you to stay but I know you won't so at least let me answer the door."

She smiled as she followed him inside. "I can't do that." She didn't mind following him because the view was quite nice. The jeans he bought in Santa Fe fit him like a glove. Once again, she thought about his last girlfriend, Monica, and wondered what could have compelled her to leave with a hedge fund manager?

Val reached the front door and looked to make sure she was behind him. He peeked through the peephole.

"Can I help you?" he asked in his grumpy, stern voice.

"Is it Red?" she asked.

"My name is Tilden," the man on the other side said.

"One second please." Val turned to look at her. "If that had been Red, I wouldn't be using my nice voice."

She laughed. "If that's your nice voice, we have some work to do on you."

"I'm fine the way I am."

She agreed. He was fine exactly the way he was, but she missed his smile. If he smiled just once the way he did when he showed up in his crazy golf attire, she could live the rest of her days in bliss.

"You are fine." She leaned in but couldn't see who was on the other side of the door.

"State your business, please," Val said in a tone much like the first—grumpy.

"Umm, I'm Tilden Cool, and I heard you need some camping equipment."

Val's whole demeanor relaxed, and he seemed to shrink a few inches. He opened the door and looked at the man standing before him.

"Did you say you have camping equipment?"

The man out front was nearly as big and tall as Val, but he didn't have that run-for-the-hills look about him. "The word that you need things is making the rounds. I wouldn't be surprised if, by dinnertime, you have enough stuff for a family of twenty to head into the mountains for a month or more."

"Are you serious?" Val asked.

Tilden nodded. "That's the way it works in Aspen Cove. It's kind of like that movie where the guy builds a baseball field in his corn crop."

Cameron stepped from behind Val. "*Field of Dreams*. I love that movie." She laid her hand on her heart. "Who am I kidding, I love Kevin Costner." She held out her hand. "I'm Cameron Ma—" Val cleared his throat. "She's Cameron."

She figured he was right. No one needed her entire resumé. She wasn't interviewing for a job.

"What did you bring us?" This was almost as good as Christmas. Better even because she had no idea what a person needed to camp but she knew Val did.

He pointed to two boxes on the porch. "There's a tent and a camp stove and a lantern and a P-38."

"What's a P-38? Is that a Porta Potty?" She breathed a sigh of relief. "And I thought we'd have to go in the bushes."

"You do have to go in the bushes," Val said. "A P-38 is a can opener."

Tilden chuckled. "But if you bring a big enough can, you can go in it."

Her shoulders sagged. "Why do people go camping when it's so inconvenient?" She stared at Tilden, but he kept his eyes on Val.

"If you don't want to go, Tilden can take his gear back home."

"This isn't for me. It's for you and we're going."

Tilden stepped back. "My job is done. Have a good trip. I think you'll be up on Doc's property. I'd hike my way up to the small lake that's there. The views are breathtaking, and you won't see a soul for days."

Val bent over and hefted a box inside the entry before getting the other. "How do we get this back to you?"

Tilden smiled. "We'll figure something out. I'm just glad it can be put to use." He turned and left just as another car pulled up, and out of the passenger seat came a young boy with two sleeping bags. "I'm David Williams." He pointed over his shoulder. "That's my mom, Louise, and she said to give you these sleeping bags." His face got all red. "I'm supposed to tell you that they are romantic bags, but don't you worry. They've been cleaned. With eight kids, my parents don't have much time for camping or romance these days."

"David Williams, get your behind back to the car, I've got a shift to pull at the diner and we need to get running." She waved at them. "I'm Louise. Have the best time in them mountains. Magic happens up there. Three of my eight kids were made in those sleeping bags."

Cameron looked up at Val. "Do you think it's safe to take them? I'm not sure I'm up for that kind of magic."

He took the bags from the boy and said thank you to Louise, who sped off as soon as David got in the car. For the next few hours, deliveries came until the hallway was filled with camping supplies. They had everything from lodging to canned meat. The last person to arrive was Doctor Parker. When Val opened the door, the old man handed him a map and a first aid kit.

"If you kids get in trouble up there, don't call me. I'm too damn old to be hiking in those parts. I've been considering selling that land because it's not getting the love it deserves."

"Would you like to come inside?" Val asked.

"No, thank you." He stared at the boxes lining the hallway. "Neither of you have time for chit chat and neither do I. Time is a precious commodity. It's like money. You have to know where you're going to spend it." He looked at them. "If I were you, I'd spend it on each other and not on an old man who wants to get home to his pot roast and The Price is Right." Doc walked out but turned around and looked at Val. Cameron watched his stern expression. "Have you kissed her yet?"

"Excuse me?"

Doc shook his head. "Youth is wasted on the young." He pointed to Cameron. "This young man likes you. I can see it, but I'm wondering if you can."

She cocked her head and looked from Doc to Val. "Oh, we're not..."

Doc waved his hand in the air. "I know you don't think you are, but I know what I see. That man cares about you, and you look at him like he's the last steak you'll eat before you go vegan."

"No." She walked to the door, shaking her head. "He's paid to care."

Doc shook his head. "Nope. He's paid to protect. He doesn't have to care." The old man turned and walked away. When Val closed the door, Cameron asked, "Is that true? Do you care?"

CHAPTER EIGHTEEN

"What I care about is getting all this sorted. If we're going camping in the morning, we need to get packed up."

Her shoulders sagged. "That's not what I asked."

"What you asked is a crazy question. It's my job to care. Doc has it all wrong." He never lied, but he did right then because sometimes lying was easier than facing the truth. He cared about Cameron a lot more than he should. Every second he was with her, he cared more. Each time she spoke, he couldn't help but stare at her lips and want to kiss them again. He needed to get out of this house and focus on something else. It was what they both needed. "Let's spread it out and see what we've got."

They worked in silence as they set out all the gear they got. It was shocking how much the people of Aspen Cove brought them. If this was what they did for total strangers, what would they do for someone they knew? Tilden was right. They had enough to set up camp for twenty if others brought their sleeping bags. Of those, they only had two. He thought back to the woman and son who brought them. Louise was banking on the fact that they would be intimate. Rampant romantic thoughts raced through his head. He imagined there was nothing sexier than making love under the stars. He needed to get these thoughts out of his head.

"We got enough. Let's pack it up." His tone was stern and unyielding, but he needed to get those sleeping bags in the back of the SUV before he justified unrolling them and making love to her on the deck.

"You sound mad." She stepped back from a box of canned goods she was sorting. "This camping trip is for you, not for me. In fact, why don't you go by yourself? You'd probably have a better time."

He'd have an easier time, but he doubted it would be better. "That isn't happening. I'm here to protect you. I'd be awful at my job if I up and left you unattended."

She stared at him, and he watched what looked like anger form. Her jaw clenched, and she fisted her hands at her side. "You know what? Outside of Red wanting to pollinate me again, I'm not in danger here."

She'd referred to him as a bee earlier, so her statement made sense, but it didn't settle well with him. "He's not getting close to you. I don't like him, and I don't trust him."

"At least he's a man I understand. I don't get you at all."

"What's there to get? You hired me to do a job, and I'm doing it. Now, let's get the car packed." He picked up the sleeping bags and started for the door until she took one from him. "I got these," he said. "You get something else."

"This one is mine, and I'll keep it for myself."

"What is wrong with you? You're not normally this difficult."

Her mouth went slack, and her eyes grew as large as golf balls. "Me? You think I'm being difficult? All you do is grump at me. I'm tired of it. All I wanted was to ensure you got a piece of your dream. You know, the one where you do something that makes you happy." She stomped her foot and hugged her sleeping bag. "You're not only a fun sucker for yourself. You suck the fun out of everything for everyone. You're an Eeyore."

"And I suppose you're Piglet?"

She made a sound like pfft. "No, I'm Tigger."

He could see that. She was full of energy and life. Having her around brought a spark of happiness to his.

"Sorry, I'm not familiar with the characters."

"You need to up your game."

"With children's books?"

She tossed the sleeping bag to the ground and walked into the kitchen, where she got a bottle of wine and the opener. She struggled to pull the cork, so he helped her open it and poured her a glass.

"I think your problem is that you never got a childhood."

He poured himself a glass. "Well, that's certainly the pot calling the kettle black."

"I was at least allowed to grow up. It might not have been a traditional childhood, but I had my fair share of childish experiences. I bet you were born a grown-up." Her words were short and clipped and a pitch above her norm. "The problem with you is that you don't know how to let go, but I'm going to help you."

"You think you can help me let go?"

She sipped her wine and smiled. "Yes. I'm positive I can help."

"Do tell, wise one. How are you going to make me let go?"

She stood as tall as she could. "You're fired. Now get the camping gear out of my living room." She walked into the living room and out the door onto the deck.

"You can't fire me. You didn't hire me."

"My money hired you; all it will take is a phone call. Don't force me to make it."

"I'm not leaving you."

She sat in the chair and stared at the lake. "You can't stay here. I don't want you here."

Her words were like a punch to his sternum or maybe a hit with the sledgehammer. Hell, he'd been shot twice, and it wasn't nearly as painful.

"I'm not leaving."

She finished her glass in two gulps and set it on the table. "If you won't leave, then I will." She stood and walked down the steps and disappeared into the night. He chased after her.

"Don't be foolish."

She stopped and turned. "I'd rather be foolish and live than be you." She was headed into town, and he knew he couldn't stop her. Cameron had come to Aspen Cove to find herself and her purpose. He wasn't sure if she'd find either, but she'd found her backbone. She was no longer the woman who'd back down under pressure.

It was just after seven and dark outside. The hoot of an owl echoed in the silence, and her pace picked up. At the edge of town, she stopped and stared ahead. He could almost see her thinking out loud, but he didn't know what her decision would be. She had two choices, the diner, or the bar. Since she'd only eaten a few crackers and cheese, he thought she'd choose the diner, but she veered to the right and walked down the street and into the bar.

He gave her a few seconds of leeway before he followed her inside. She took the last seat at the end of the bar, and he took a seat next to Doc.

The older man looked up at him. "Perfect timing." He pointed to his empty mug. "I could use a refill." He flagged down the man behind the bar. "Cannon, this young man is buying my next beer."

Val didn't argue. He knew he owed Doc for many things, like a house call and the use of his land if they ever made it camping.

"I'll pick up Doc's bill." He nodded toward Cameron. "And hers." He imagined Cameron hadn't considered how she'd pay for her drinks because she didn't have any money.

"What'll you have?" Cannon asked.

He almost said water because he rarely drank on the job, but Cameron had fired him, so he wasn't technically on the clock. "Something dark and cold."

"Like his personality," Cameron called out from the end of the bar.

"Trouble in paradise, son?"

"Paradise? My life is a living nightmare."

Cannon put two beers in front of them and slid a glass of wine down the bar to Cameron. "Wait until you have a wife and a kid. It's pure bliss with a side of a nightmare."

"Well, that isn't likely to happen. I'm married to my job, and that's nightmare enough. Although, tonight, she fired me."

"Sage has tried to get rid of me many times, but I'm like a sticky booger. You can't shake me off." Cannon pushed off the counter and walked into the bar to pick up empty mugs and pitchers.

Val caught sight of Red sitting with two women in the corner, but his attention was focused on Cameron. All he wanted to do was go over and give that man a beatdown.

"I wouldn't act on the impulse, young man," Doc said.

"He needs to have his ass beat."

"I don't disagree, but I find that Karma often delivers the beatings better." Doc took a drink of his beer, leaving the foam

141

bubbling on his bushy mustache. "What's going on with you and Cameron?"

"She says I'm a fun sucker and an Eeyore."

"Are you?"

He picked up his mug and drank deeply. The cold felt terrific as the bubbles made their way down.

"I have a serious job, and I can't take my eye off the ball to have fun. It doesn't go well for anyone when I drop the ball."

"There's a saying about all work and no play making you a dull boy."

"It's true." He'd been working for years and lost his ability to have fun.

"Then let your hair down for a second and have some fun."

Cameron got up and headed in Red's direction. Val stiffened and started after her, but Doc grabbed his arm.

"Let karma take this one. She doesn't look like a woman on the prowl. She's a woman with a growl."

Against his instincts, he watched as Cameron walked over to Red. She addressed the woman, leaned in, and whispered something in Red's ear. When he smiled and nodded, she pulled back her fist and punched him in the nose. Then she returned, sat down, and gulped her wine before ordering another.

Val couldn't wait to hear what went down but figured he was close to being on the wrong side of her other fist. He stayed put and silent.

Doc leaned in and said, "It's obvious that you like the girl. What's holding you back? Are you afraid of her? She packs a punch."

They looked at Red who was sopping up his bloody nose mess with a wad of napkins.

"She doesn't scare me in that way. I can't get involved with a client."

Doc reached over and cuffed him in the ear. "You need to pay attention. She fired you, son. She set you free to have some fun. What will you do about it?"

Doc was right. They were no longer in a professional relationship. Someone selected a song from the jukebox, and while dancing wasn't one of Val's strong points, he approached Cameron and asked her to dance.

"Why?"

"Because it's fun." It was a lame excuse, but he knew it would work. For some reason, Cameron's focus was on him having fun.

"Do you like to dance?"

He shrugged. "I'd like to dance with you." He took her hand in his. "What do you say? Let's have some fun."

"I don't know. My hand hurts because men are hardheaded."

He lifted her knuckles to his mouth and kissed them. "We're all idiots."

"At least we agree on something."

"Care to tell me what happened?"

"I was just confirming his level of assholery when I asked if he'd ditch the girls and he said yes. For him, he's always interested in the highest bidder."

"I'm guessing by your reaction that he said yes? Did you consider leaving with him?"

She shook her head. "I'm not an asshole, and he is definitely not the highest bidder. Didn't you ask me to dance?"

She followed him to the small dance floor, where he pulled her into his arms and held her as they swayed to the music.

"I think this is supposed to be a fast dance song."

He kissed the top of her head. "Maybe, but with you, I want to take things slowly and savor every moment."

She pressed her head to his chest and sighed. "What are you up to?"

"Just following your advice. I'm learning how to have fun, but I need a teacher. Would you care to go camping with me?"

"You don't work for me anymore."

He nodded. "I know, so come with me because you want to."

She snuggled more tightly against him. "That was why I was always going. I just wanted to be with you."

He breathed her in. She was sunshine and rainbows, and he knew the next few days would change everything. The question was, how much?

CHAPTER NINETEEN

Cameron woke to the smell of bacon and eggs. She woke to that smell last Christmas when she stayed at her mother's house for the holidays. Though she grew up in a non-traditional upbringing, her mother always did everyday things like making her breakfast.

She climbed out of bed and padded her way into the kitchen, where Val stood in front of the stove.

"What are you doing?"

"I'm making breakfast." He pointed to the table in front of the window. "Have a seat. I've got a cup of coffee brewing for you. One sweetener and cream, right?"

She nodded. "What's wrong with you? You're being nice."

He placed her coffee in front of her. "I'm always nice, but today, I'm trying your kind of nice."

She picked up the mug and took a sip. It was perfect. This whole scene was perfect, and she never trusted that.

"How long will this last?"

He plated her eggs and bacon and put them in front of her. "I don't know. It's a first for me." He sat across from her and watched her as she stared at her eggs. "Don't worry. I didn't poison them."

"I didn't think that. I was just wondering why you were so kind after I fired you. You're still fired in case you were wondering." She remembered the night before when they danced, drank wine, and walked home. She may have been a little tipsy, but she couldn't remember rehiring him.

"I know, and I'm quite pleased about it. Lucky isn't happy, but I can understand why. He cares about you and wants you safe. I told him I'd do my best to keep you out of trouble, but I had no real control."

"You realize you never did, right? You being in charge was a façade." She was pushing his buttons to see if his primary personality would engage, but to his credit, he sat there and smiled.

"I think the level of control comes down to the client. Most people like it when you take charge." He took a bite of a piece of bacon. "It releases them from making decisions, but I realize that someone like you needs to make a decision to feel in control of their life, and I also know that feeling in control is important."

"I appreciate that. When do we leave?"

He cut into his eggs and took a bite. When he swallowed, he said. "That's up to you."

She smiled. "How about after we eat."

"Perfect. The car is packed." He finished his breakfast, got up, and put his plate in the dishwasher. "I'll be on the deck waiting. Just let me know when you're ready."

She decided to give him a taste of his medicine. "I'll be in the car in ten minutes. If you're not there, I'm leaving without you."

He lifted a brow and smiled. "I'll be there."

As soon as he walked outside, she gobbled up the rest of

her breakfast and raced to her room to change. She didn't know what people wore for camping but figured jeans, shorts, and a few T-shirts would be fine. She got dressed, pulled on her sneakers, and rushed to the car so she'd be waiting there when he arrived.

At the ten-minute mark, he strolled back to the house and locked the door. When he sat in the driver's seat, he turned. "Oh, I thought you'd be driving since you threatened to leave me behind."

She buckled in. "I can barely drive on the road. Imagine what that would look like if I went four-wheeling."

"True, you're not ready for off-road driving." He put the car in gear and started down the road. "Do you have everything you need?"

She lifted her hands in the air. "How would I know? I've never been camping and don't know what I need. If I don't have it, I guess I don't need it."

He chuckled. "Or if you don't have it, you don't need it until you realize you do, and then it's too late." He turned onto a road that led past the cemetery. It wound back and forth into the mountains. "Doc's map was pretty clear. It said to follow this road until it ends, and then we're on foot."

"Like as in hiking?"

"It's the only way to get back into the woods and the lake."

She looked behind her but couldn't see the supplies because they were tucked behind the back seats. "We have to haul all that stuff by foot."

He reached over and patted her hand. "I packed only the necessities. Bowie brought two rucksacks by, and I've packed them to the hilt with everything I think we'll need."

She stared at him. The man must be out of his mind. "I'm not carrying a rucksack."

He smiled. "You are if you want to sleep in a tent or a

sleeping bag."

"Can't we camp next to where we park? I mean, it's all about sleeping outdoors, right?"

He continued driving. "If that were the case, then we could have slept on the deck." He turned toward her. "Are you having second thoughts? I can turn around if you want to back out."

She shook her head. She was a lot of things, but she wasn't a quitter. "Nope, I said I'd come, and I'm here. Let's do this thing." The whole point was to make Val happy, but she didn't realize she'd have to make herself miserable. "What exactly do you get out of camping?"

"It's one with nature. Out here, nothing bothers you. There are no schedules or expectations."

She liked the sound of that. Her life was about schedules and expectations. Maybe she needed this as much as he did.

When he pulled up to a split rail fence, Val said. "And this is as far as the car can take us."

She rolled her shoulder and stretched her arms. "How much does my pack weigh."

He got out of the car and walked around to open the door for her. "A hundred pounds or so."

She felt like the ground opened up and swallowed her. "A hundred pounds?" How was she supposed to carry something that weighed nearly as much as she did? "Okay, I'll figure it out."

"I'll help." He rounded the SUV and opened the back. Inside was a large rucksack, and next to it was a smaller backpack. Val grabbed the smaller bag and handed it to her. "I'll do the heavy lifting."

"That's not fair." She stared at the heft of the bag and said a silent prayer of thanks. "I feel like you're getting the short end of the stick in this deal." '

He helped her put on the backpack. Despite its smaller size, it was heavy. "What's in this?"

"The camp stove and canned goods. If we got separated, I didn't want you to get hangry." He buckled the front harness, which took some of the pressure off her shoulders. "I made sure to put the P-38 inside too."

"That's so sweet. What if I don't want to share?"

"It goes both ways. I have a tent and sleeping bags. It will get mighty cold when the sun sets."

"I suppose I can share." She smiled. "Do we have one tent or two?"

He walked toward the fence and climbed over, waiting for her to do the same. "This isn't the Ritz; we aren't entitled to a suite of rooms. It's one tent, but we have two sleep bags."

She hadn't considered their sleeping arrangements, but it was too late to change anything. "Do you snore?"

"I don't know. You'll have to tell me. Do you?"

She grinned. "I sound like a freight train."

"Can't wait."

They walked for over an hour into the wilderness. Except for a few birds and bunnies, there wasn't any wildlife to speak of. Cameron wasn't sure if she should be grateful or disappointed. And then they left the tree line, and a lake and field of wildflowers were in front of her—something inside her burst at the seams. Tears cascaded down her face. She'd never been so happy.

"Are you okay?"

"I'm so happy to be here." She ran toward the water like a bear was chasing her. At the edge, she dropped her backpack and kicked off her shoes. "Is it safe to go in?"

He dropped his rucksack, and before she knew it, he was stripping down to his boxers. He dove headfirst into the water. "Are you coming in?"

CHAPTER TWENTY

Val watched the indecision on her face. "It would make me happy."

"Is it cold?"

"Yes." The water was frigid, but that was to be expected in a mountain lake that got its water from snow melt. While cold, it was invigorating. "But it feels amazing." He was where his feet couldn't touch the bottom, and so he trod water and waited. "You'll never know if you like it if you don't try."

She glanced around as if looking for paparazzi. Sadly, that was her life, and he couldn't imagine living under the scrutiny of the fickle public. One day they loved you, and the next, they didn't. Fortunately for Cameron, she'd never given them a reason to turn on her.

"Fine, but only because it will make you happy, and making you happy is what this camping trip is about."

She started to undress, and he couldn't take his eyes off her. She was Hollywood slim but not in a traditional way. She had all the right curves in the right places, and everything about her looked God-given and natural from this distance, which was odd since most stars were nipped, tucked, and enhanced. When she got to her underwear and bra, she stood on the shore and waited as if she needed an invitation.

"Are you coming or not."

"I'm not a great swimmer."

He laughed. "Then why do you have a pool?" He'd seen the lap pool while they were arguing about his rules.

"It came with the penthouse, and it's pretty. I like being by the water."

"I won't let you drown." He walked forward but only until he was hip deep. To come out of the water any farther would expose how much she affected him. Despite the cold water, heat rushed through him when he saw her nearly naked. He tried to convince himself that his reaction to her wasn't about her but simply because she was a beautiful woman and seeing her in her silk underwear and bra would affect any hot-blooded hetero man. Men were programmed to respond to boobs and butts. He was reacting as any man would.

She walked to the water's edge with her arms wrapped around her chest, but he'd already seen what was there, and that vision would never leave his brain. She dipped a toe in the water and moved away from it. "It's freezing."

"I told you it was cold. Be brave."

She eyed him suspiciously, then dropped her hands and ran toward the water, throwing herself in entirely once she got to her knees. She came up spitting and sputtering and flailing her hands.

He was only a few feet from her and closed the distance. She reached for him, and he picked her up, her feet wrapped around his waist. An unexpected groan came from deep inside. He was in heaven and hell at the same time.

"You're right. It's invigorating." She clung to him like he was a life preserver, and given that she wasn't a strong swimmer, he figured that's what he was.

"It's darn right cold. My man parts have receded, and I may not see them for weeks."

She wiggled against him. "Nope, they're there and seem to work fine. You probably can't feel them."

"Oh, I feel them." He moved into deeper water.

"Do you think there are fish in here?" she asked.

"Definitely."

She pushed off of him and giggled. "I bet they're looking around and wondering who we are."

"Can you imagine?" He never considered what a fish might think. "They have small brains, and all they think about is survival."

She moved to her back and floated at the surface. "Do you think the wildlife drink from this water?" As if she had just considered water, she gasped. "What are we going to drink?"

"This water." He splashed the water forward

She sank until her body was underwater, and only her head broke the surface. "We have to drink the bath water?"

He laughed. "We'll boil it."

"Sounds awful."

"Lots of things sound awful until you try them." He swam over to her. "Are you enjoying the swim?"

"Yes, but I fear I'm done." Her teeth chattered. "Are my lips turning blue?"

They were, so he nodded toward the shore. "Let's catch the sun before it slips behind the peak in a few hours. We have to set up camp and gather wood for a fire."

"I'm glad I'm doing this with you."

His chest got tight. "Oh yeah? Why?"

She paddled past him. "Because I don't know how to make a fire. I'd surely perish the first night."

"And I thought it was because you loved my sunny disposition."

She walked out of the water and onto the shore. "Oh, you're not so bad. Your bark is worse than your bite."

"How do you know?" he asked as he walked out of the water. "You've never experienced my bite." He strode right for her and leaned over to nip her shoulder.

She squealed and turned around to face him. When their eyes met, it was game over. Those damn eyes were like magical orbs that made him lose all common sense. Starting something with her was wrong, but mostly because it would never go anywhere. She was from Hollywood, and he was from where his next job happened. But he'd be damned if he could help himself.

"I'm going to kiss you again. If that's not something you want, let's dress and head back to the car."

She stumbled back, and he caught her by the shoulders. "The car? Why?"

He rubbed one palm over his face. "Because if I have to be out here with you, and I can't taste those lips again, it will be pure torture."

She licked her lips and looked up at him. "You like my lips?"

"You taste like fresh berries and happiness."

She laughed. "How can someone taste like happiness? What does that taste like?"

He leaned down until his lips brushed hers. "You. It tastes like you."

"Then kiss me."

He covered her mouth and her lips parted. He loved how easily she let him in. It was a gift, and he'd be damned if he wouldn't accept everything she offered.

The kiss could have lasted all night and he wanted it to, but a breeze kicked up, and gooseflesh rose on her skin. Reluctantly, he ended the kiss and stepped away.

"Let's get you dressed. You have to be freezing."

"I am so far from freezing it's funny. You sure know how to heat a girl."

"So, my bite is pretty good."

"You're right. A person can taste like something other than a flavor." She licked her lips. "You taste like hope."

"Hope?" He grabbed his jeans and tugged them on. He'd regret the wet boxers later, but the discomfort would remind him of how stupid it was to get involved with a client. Sure, she'd fired him, but he felt he needed to protect her. Was that his built-in bodyguard speaking, or something deeper? If it were the latter, he knew someone would get hurt because there was no hope for them.

"Yes. Kissing you makes me feel hopeful."

He wanted to grab and fill her with hope, but that wasn't wise. In a few weeks, she'd return to her life, and he'd return to his. "Whatever this is between us isn't a forever thing, right?"

She snapped back as if he'd slapped her, and he wanted to reach out and hold her, but it was essential to set the rules for whatever this was before it went further.

She tugged on her jeans and a T-shirt and crammed her sockless feet into her tennis shoes. "Don't worry, Val. You're just a distraction. You're not even my type."

If she wanted to wound, she'd had a direct hit to his heart, but then again, he'd fired first. "Okay, I just don't want you to get hurt."

"Do you have a habit of hurting women?" She picked up her backpack and looked around. "Where are we setting up camp?" The last sentence came out chopped and warbling. He watched as she swiped at her eyes. "The water must be salty. My eyes burn."

"Must be." He wasn't going to break the news that it was

fresh water. He felt like shit for hurting her feelings, but some things were better off not explored.

He found a flat, clear piece of land near the tree line and began setting up camp. The first thing out of the rucksack was the tent. It was one of the flexible pole types that were easy to put together, and he had it set up in less than fifteen minutes.

He hated that their moment of passion imploded because his logical mind needed to dot the i's and cross the t's. But he knew how this ended.

He gathered rocks to create a fire pit.

"What should I do?" Her whole demeanor was smaller, as if his words had diminished her.

He dropped the rocks and reached for her. "Come here." He held out his arms and she stepped into them. "I'm sorry. You're right. I'm a fun sucker." As unflattering as that sounded, it was true. He'd taken a special moment and turned it into something negative. Since when did attraction for one another become bad? "Let's go back and start that over, but before we do, I was thinking about the aftermath and not the moment."

"Are you afraid I'm going to break your heart?"

He refused to admit it, but yes.

CHAPTER TWENTY-ONE

She laid her head against his shirt and breathed him in. He should have smelled like sweat and lake water, but he smelled like he tasted, like hope and joy. Maybe it was because she'd been so isolated in her life, and now, this man had shared himself with her, or at least his lips for a moment, and she liked them. This wasn't a grand love affair. It was a detour from their regular lives, and on detours, wasn't it customary to take in the scenery? Something told her it was almost criminal if she didn't.

"You like rules, right?" She stepped back and looked up at him. He had beautiful green eyes. While hers were extremely rare, people didn't realize how rare green eyes were too. She'd once read that only two percent of the population had them, and his were stunning. They were the color of pine needles kissed by the sun.

"You know me. I love a good rule."

She placed her hands on his chest. "Okay, then I'm making a rule that you'll like. We will have fun; if that means our lips and bodies meet from time to time, that's all part of the enjoyment. This isn't about love." Her thoughts went to Red for a nanosecond. "We aren't looking for that, right?"

He shook his head. "I haven't had much luck in that department."

"Me either." She wrapped her arms around him. "I propose we enjoy each other with no expectations of anything more. That seems fair and prudent."

He hugged her close to him. "I think that's a good idea. Can I kiss you again?"

"If you don't, I'll be disappointed." She lifted on tiptoes and pressed her lips to his. It was a sweet and sensual kiss, and while she tried to keep her mind and heart detached, it was impossible. She knew she was lying to herself. She'd fall head over heels for Val, and when they separated, she'd be heartbroken but wasn't it better to have loved and lost than never to have loved at all? At least, that's what Tennyson said.

They kissed until a bird flew over and screeched as if reminding them to get their chores done.

He broke the kiss, "We should finish setting up camp." He looked around. "I'll finish getting the fire pit ready if you gather some kindling and fallen wood."

"I can do that." She'd never been afraid of hard work. Her mother always told her the harder she worked, the luckier she'd get, and she supposed that's why she was still employable. She was always on time, never complained, and did what people expected. While she grew tired of the monotony and the rules, maybe those rules she chose to follow made her what she was today. As she walked the forest edge, picking up small sticks, she considered how life changed when her perspective changed. She'd bristled at the rules, but in hindsight, they'd always kept her on the right track.

When she brought an armload of sticks back, she found Val sawing wood with what looked like a bow. "What is that?"

He held up a branch that had a metal wire attached to it. "It's a bow saw. The wire was in a survival kit, and I whipped up the bow to make it easier.

"You're like that guy on TV who could make a bomb out of a Q-tip and a match."

He laughed. "MacGyver? You'd need more than that."

"Do you know how?"

He continued to cut wood. "If I told you I'd have to—"

"Kill me. I know, I've heard it all before."

"No, I'd have to keep you, and that's not part of the rules."

"Damn rules." She saw he'd muscled over two large rocks. "Primitive seating?"

He nodded. "Better than the ground." He nodded toward her pack and his. "You want to unpack the groceries?"

She unbuckled her bag, dumped out the contents, and squealed with delight. "We're having s'mores?" She hadn't had one since they filmed a remake of *Parent Trap*, and she got to have one on the set. She sorted the cans out and saw they had lots of chili and soup, which meant they wouldn't starve. There was even a can of asparagus and peaches and in a plastic container were eggs which made her heart feel happy and full.

"I figured tonight we'd have chili and s'mores for dessert. Tomorrow, I'll make us scrambled eggs and Spam. Then we'll try our hand at fishing. If we catch something, we'll eat it; if not, we'll have soup."

She pointed to the four cans of chili. "Or we'll eat chili again."

"Or that." The sun was setting when he started the fire. He taught her how to stack the kindling so the flame would catch, and when it did, she felt like she'd contributed, even if it was only through her excitement.

"What now?" She stared at the flames, mesmerized by the movement and the color.

"Now, we relax and enjoy and talk and kiss." He took the rock beside her and gave her a peck on the lips before reaching for a can of chili and the small pan in her sack. He pulled out what he called a P-38 and quickly opened the can with a back-and-forth motion. "Is there anything you wanted to be besides an actor or a coffee shop owner?"

She thought about that and laughed. "I wanted to be a princess, but then Megan Markle got the only remaining prince worth marrying. After that, my royal dreams were dashed. What about you? Anything other than security sex god or mountain man?"

"Sex god?"

She could feel the heat of her blush. "Well, if you make love with the same passion as you kiss, then own it."

He stirred the chili. "I wanted to be a race car driver."

"Why didn't you do that."

He sighed. "You know. There are the dreams we have and the reality we get."

"I know it all too well." They both sat staring at the fire until their meal was bubbling in the pan. She gathered two metal bowls and spoons, and they split the meal.

After the meal, he washed the pan in the lake and returned with water to boil.

She was still unsure if she wanted to drink it but felt that trying at night when she couldn't see it would make it more palatable.

When Val finished boiling the water, he poured two cups and pulled a tea bag out of thin air. "I thought you might enjoy a cup of tea."

His thoughtfulness touched her. He'd brought little pieces of joy for her to appreciate.

"You are so sweet."

He smiled. "Don't let that get out."

She made a button her lip motion. "Your secret is safe with me."

The rest of the night, they sat by the fire eating s'mores, drinking tea, and sharing stories. By bedtime, she had a good idea of who Val was, and it wasn't the man he presented. Sure, he was solid and capable, but there was a vulnerable side to him that she imagined he didn't show many people, and somehow, he had let her in.

She yawned and stretched. "I'm tired and ready for bed."

He looked back at the tent. "You go first and pick your sleeping bag. I'll bank the fire and make sure we're set for the night."

"Are you sure?" She didn't want to saddle him with the work, but she wasn't sure how helpful she could be.

"I got this. Get changed, and I'll be in in a few minutes."

At the mention of getting changed, she gasped. "I didn't bring anything to sleep in."

He grinned. "This camping trip gets better every minute."

"You're awful."

"I'm honest. A hot woman who has nothing to wear to bed? That's a win in my book."

"You think I'm hot?"

He pointed to the fire. "Like a blue flame."

She trotted off, feeling as high as a loose helium balloon. When she got into the tent, she saw he'd laid both sleeping bags out, side by side. Next to them was a stack of their clothes. Her pile had extra pants, underwear, socks, and a couple of shirts. Val was a light packer, but he had an extra shirt inside his bag—a shirt that would be perfect for her to wear to bed.

"Hey, Val?"

He poked his head inside the tent and saw her looking at his clothes. He smiled, which made her heart take off. "Help yourself." He backed out and let the flap fall into place.

"You're the best."

"Promise you'll keep that to yourself too?"

"Why do you want everyone to think you're the bad guy?"

CHAPTER TWENTY-TWO

"It's part of the persona." With his back to the tent, clothes rustling, and sleeping bags crinkling, a whoosh of Cameron-scented air swirled around him. He didn't know how she still smelled like she'd bathed in flowers, but she did. In the distance, an owl hooted as if telling him to douse the dying flames, and when he tossed the bucket of lake water onto the charred logs, the embers hissed as if they were offended that he was trading their warmth for hers.

"Does that persona thing work for you?"

He waited until the steam evaporated, making sure nothing left behind would catch fire before entering the lantern-lit tent to find Cameron dressed in his pink polo shirt. He'd be damned if that wasn't the hottest thing he'd ever seen in his lifetime.

"I thought you'd choose the gray T-shirt?"

She sat up and touched the collar. "Don't you dislike this shirt? I tried to pick the one you'd miss least."

The tent was six inches shorter than him, so he was hunched over. "That might be my favorite shirt now."

"You are such a flirt."

"It's the truth." He pulled his shirt over his head and folded it, tucking it under the pile of clean clothes. When he glanced at Cameron, she was staring at him or, more accurately, his shoulder.

"Does it hurt?" And while he was feet above her, she reached her fingertips toward his shoulder as if she could easily touch him. Having her hands on him was all he could think about, so he fell to his knees, and she touched the gunshot wound. Not once had he been grateful for the injury until that second. "It took out a chunk of skin."

"I supposed better a flesh wound than having it embedded in my skin."

"You need to find less hazardous clients."

"I'm getting too old for this shit." Her fingertips left the scar and danced over his skin. First his collarbone and then his sternum. He closed his eyes as she moved through his chest hair. He imagined she was drawing words, but then she moved on to the hills and valleys of his upper stomach until his jeans halted her progress.

"Sorry, that was forward of me, but you have a great body. I imagine it's hard ... to keep it in shape?"

He settled his hand over hers. Not to stop her already stilled progress, but to keep her close to him. Something happened when Cameron touched him. His world went silent, and he loved the stillness she brought, despite their chaotic existence together. It was as if the moment her skin connected to his, everything stopped, and he waited on bated breath to see what was next. Even now, as he held her hand against his stomach, not even the owl dared to speak.

"You know where this is going, right?"

She smiled in the lantern's glow, and it was as if the sun had lit up the tiny space. "I know where I hope it will go."

He reached below her hand to tug the button of his jeans free. "Show me where you want it to go."

Her hands disappeared under the down-filled bag and appeared again when she tugged the hem of the shirt over her head. He couldn't take his eyes off her as the pink material skated up her tummy and ribs. The fabric resisted at her chest and then seemed to give way as she tugged it past her breasts.

They mesmerized him. It wasn't like he hadn't seen a pair. He'd seen plenty but none as perfectly round and eager for his touch. She cleared her head, and long blonde locks fell over her shoulders. He was about to ask for permission to touch her, but she threw herself at him, and when their skin touched, it was game on and game over for his heart.

"You're overdressed for this job." They fell to the ground, and she fumbled with his zipper.

"Let me fix that." It took him no time to shimmy out of his jeans, boxers, and socks. The air outside cooled while their passion heated. Cameron was like an outdoor adventure on her own. There was so much to explore. He started with her lips, and she still tasted like berries, or maybe that was just a flavor he associated with her, but he loved the way her tongue danced with his. The way she groaned when he nibbled her lip and the way her body sought his when he sucked on her tongue. He pulled back. "Is anything off limits?"

She took several breaths. "You mean like breath play and bondage? Will I need a safe word?"

His head snapped back. This was America's sweetheart talking about BDSM and secret phrases. "No, I was just wondering if..." He wasn't sure how to answer that. Had he pegged her wrong? He certainly didn't mind a curious woman who had no problem exploring sex with him, but safe words? All he wanted to do was make love to her. That thought rocked his world. He felt love for her. No matter how much he tried to blame his feeling on other things like a crisis event or her eyes, Cameron had shown him compassion and care when she could have shown him her moody side. He wasn't sure she had one. What she'd call her worst day was the best day for most of the women he'd been with. "Can I make love to you?"

Her expression got soft at first, then questioning. "But I thought this was just for now with no expectations. Calling it love means something."

He knew she was right, but he couldn't help himself. "Have you done method acting?"

"Not really but I hear it's a good way to embody a character fully."

"How about we both treat this weekend like a method-acting experience? I'd love to know what it feels like to be loved by you."

She gnawed on her lip. "What about you?"

He smiled. "I'm no actor, but I will love you like you're mine." His heart, usually just a muscle that moved the blood through his system, squeezed and tightened and then did a flip. It was the strangest sensation because it seemed to heat up after all that. He looked down to make sure it wasn't glowing through his skin.

"I have condoms."

She laughed. "Were you a Boy Scout? Don't they have that motto about being prepared or something?"

He laid down and pulled her on top of him. Everywhere her body touched was instantly turned into a pleasure point.

"I have no idea, I was never a scout, but I'll pretend to be if you think it would make me sexier."

"If you got any sexier, I'd have to bottle you up and sell you. We could both retire."

He rolled over, pinning her under him. "Where would we live?"

"Right here." She giggled.

"In this tent?" He kissed her collarbone and then licked at the hollow of her neck. A groan snuck past her lips, and he repeated the action on the other side until he got the same response.

Her breath quickened as her hands slowly explored his back, settling on the top curve of his ass.

"I've loved it out here, but maybe that's because I love you."

There went his heart again. He knew this was an act, but he loved how it felt when she said the words.

"I bet Doc would sell us the land." He kissed her jaw, her cheek, and then her lips, but he only brushed them and moved on to the hollow below her neck. "He mentioned that he was too old to be caring for it. Would you want a mansion?"

She ran her tongue up his neck and grazed his jawline with her teeth. "No, a small cabin big enough to house our two kids and us."

The pressure inside him was building, and the mention of their children made him want to plant them inside her that night. Every part of him throbbed with the need to release. "Two," he barely breathed out.

"Yes, two boys like their father." She shifted so his hardness sat right at her apex. All it would take was one thrust, and they'd be one.

"What if I wanted a girl who looked like their mother? Hair like spun gold and eyes like amethysts?"

"Then we'd have to have three." Her hips rocked until his very tip slid inside—pure torture. Absolute heaven.

"Please." The word spilled from her lips like a plea. "I need you inside me."

"I like that idea." She was killing him. Every time her body moved, it sent an electrical impulse straight to his junk. His inner sixteen-year-old boy was ready to dive in, but his mature man self told him to slow down and enjoy the expedition. Every journey had several paths to get from the place he was to where he wanted to be. There was always a shorter path, but he'd always loved the scenic route. "You won't need a safe word. You'll always be safe with me, but for shits and giggles, what would yours be if you chose one?"

"Banana pants," she blurted before cupping his back end and pulling him forward. "And yours?"

He shifted his body, so it wasn't over before it began. "Rules."

She reached up and twisted his nipple, which should have hurt, but it only fueled him with more passion. He rose, adjusted the lantern light, so it was a soft glow, and reached for his pants to get a condom. Hard as the boulder they'd sat on, it made it easy to roll the condom on. She spread her legs showing her eagerness to receive him, but she'd have to wait because this journey did not start and end at her core.

He shimmied his way to her feet, kissed her ankles and calves, and spent endless minutes worshipping her thighs. In the dim light, he surveyed the land and found landmarks he wanted to visit again, the constellation of freckles that looked just like the little dipper with the handle pointing straight to her sex. Not that he'd ever get lost, but if he did, he wanted to have her completely mapped out.

He loved how she squirmed when he licked his way to her core, how she clenched her thighs around his head. He wasn't sure if she was trying to hinder his progress or keep him there. It turned out the latter because she gripped his hair and asked for more when he shifted. While her mouth tasted like berries, the rest of her was like icing that coated his tongue with sweetness. If he were starving, he could live on her alone. Who was he kidding? He was starving—starving for love and his place in the world, and he'd found it. It was right there with Cameron in their make-believe world in the mountains.

As her thighs shook, he remembered the one thing she wanted before she died, an orgasm with a real man. "Time to check off another bucket list item."

She lifted her head. "What?"

"Hold on, baby, it's about to get real." He covered her with his mouth and sucked. She stilled and held her breath until he was sure she'd pass out, and then her whole body shook, and the most beautiful sound filled the air. It was his name, as if the wind had caught it and circled their bodies with her voice. He didn't relent until she squirmed and pleaded for him to stop.

"Banana—"

She didn't need a safe word. He was there with her. He moved up until he was perfectly aligned and slid inside her heat. There wasn't a cabin, mansion, or place on earth that he'd rather be than inside her.

His teenager was back, wanting to rush to the climax. He breathed deep, desperate to get himself under control. He was reaching for his climax as Cameron was coming down from hers.

"You are good for me," she said. She lifted her legs and wrapped them around his waist, pulling him deeper. Sweat built on his brow and he thrust inside her racing to the finish line. When he got there, he stilled and let every emotion that he'd never allowed himself wash over him. His whole body shuddered before he collapsed on top of her. In the afterglow, she skimmed her fingers across his skin and kissed him slowly and lovingly like the wife she was pretending to be. Everything about this moment was everything he wanted. That was the funniest thing about life; you often don't get the things you want because you don't know that it's your right to want more or ask for them. He held her tight as he slid out of her body and shifted to her side. Cameron Madden didn't know that what she was pretending was what he was aiming to get. He didn't know how it would happen, but she was his, and it wasn't only for pretend.

CHAPTER TWENTY-THREE

She was never into method acting because it required the actor to fully immerse themselves into a role, and her parts didn't need that kind of commitment, but if it was as easy to do as her deal with Val, she'd had to give it more thought. They'd woken early that morning and made love again, only this time she told him she loved him. If he wanted to do the whole shebang, it came with words.

The only problem was that she felt something real and profound in her chest when she said them. She had to remind herself that this was not for real. If it had been for real, she'd hit the lottery.

"Are you paying attention?" Val asked. He'd brought two stumps from the forest floor to the water's edge. "Worms are the way to go if we're trying to catch trout."

He'd dug up a dozen worms after they ate scrambled eggs and fried Spam. She'd never had Spam, it had never appealed to her, but when Val got up and made her breakfast over an open fire, she would have eaten anything, including those gross wiggly worms he was trying to teach her to put on hooks.

Nothing screamed sexy like a shirtless Val hovering over a frying pan making her a meal.

"It seems cruel to the worm." She watched him thread it on the hook and cast his line into the lake.

"That seems cruel, but eating the fish we catch doesn't? It's all a food chain thing. At least the fish got to have an amazing final meal."

She stood and cast her line into the water with an empty hook. "How about this ... if I catch a fish with an empty hook, then it was meant to be. If not, I didn't have to torture a worm in the process."

He chuckled. "You're never catching a fish with an empty hook."

"You're probably right, but being my soulmate, you'll share, right?"

"You bet. Everything I have is yours, baby."

She smiled and took a seat on the stump. She couldn't stand if she wanted to since those words made her weak in the knees. "Thanks for teaching me how to cast." That part was the best because he folded his body around hers, and they moved as one.

"You're a quick learner."

She frowned. "Yes, too quick." She got the hang of it right away and missed the heat of his body next to hers. The tip of her pole bent, and she leaped to her feet. "I've got a bite."

Val shook his head. "You're probably caught up on something."

The pole bobbed again. "Are you sure?"

"If you caught a fish on an empty hook, I'm never letting you go. That's some magic." He stood next to her. "Yank it back, and let's pull it in slowly."

She rose and did as he said. As the line pulled in, she struggled with the weight of what was on the other side. "It's a fish." She tugged, stretched, and stepped back until a large trout flopped onto the land. "Oh my God. The universe wants us to eat."

Val picked up the fish and held it out. "Holy hell, that's at least a foot or more."

"Will it feed us?"

"Are you going to share?" he asked.

"Yes, love. Everything I have is yours." She lifted and pressed her lips to his. "Is it weird that I feel..."

"You feel what?" He lifted a brow and waited.

"All hot and needy."

Val grinned. "Wow, catching a fish turns you on."

She nodded and lowered her head. "Does that make it weird?"

He strung a line through the fish's mouth, secured it to a nearby log, and pointed to the tent. "I think that's the hottest thing I've heard in ... forever. I'll race you." He took off toward the tent while she took her time. It's not always a race to the end, and she knew that. For this trip, she was going to relish every second. And if part of that journey was making her sexy security detail wait, and finding him naked and ready, then she would enjoy every microsecond of the experience.

When she pulled back the flap, he was completely nude. She'd had a lot of leading men in her life, but Val was the sexiest.

"Are you having second thoughts?" he asked.

She shook her head. "How many condoms did you bring?"

He sank into the down sleeping bag. "Not nearly enough."

"What if we didn't use them?"

He eyed her. "Is that wise?"

Her hand came to her mouth. "Oh my. I've misled you. What I meant was, why don't we do other stuff? Like—"

He tugged her inside, and before she hit the ground, she swore he had her naked. It wasn't true, but she felt naked with him all the time, and it wasn't simply sans clothes. He saw past her skin to her soul.

"Did you like that last night?"

"I've never—"

"You can't say that anymore." He fist-pumped the air. "Your first!" He tugged her shoes off first and moved on to her pants. The cool air hit her tender flesh but was quickly replaced by the heat of his tongue. They pleasured each other for what seemed like a lifetime. He brought her to the edge and back so many times her entire body shook with need.

She tortured him in a like manner until he begged her to release him from his agony, and she did. Much to her surprise, he didn't leave her hanging like many a man would, but he took her to heights of passion she didn't think were possible.

They lay naked in each other's arms until she was sure she heard the whinny of a horse. "Did you hear that?"

Val groggily lifted his head. "Hear what?"

"Someone's here."

Distinctive hoofbeats neared the tent, and Val sprung into action. He was on his feet, and in his pants so fast it made her dizzy. "Stay here." He pulled on his shirt and slipped on his shoes before grabbing a gun from his bag.

"You brought a weapon?" She hadn't considered they'd be in danger in the wild. In her mind, there might be issues with wildlife but not humans.

"Get dressed and stay here." He tucked the gun into the waistband of his pants and disappeared outside.

"State your business," he said in his deep don't mess with

me voice. It was a tone that sent shivers down her spine, so she imagined it would scare the hell out of anyone he confronted.

Not wanting anyone to find her only wearing the blush of an Oscar-worthy orgasm, she fished around the tent for her clothes. Cameron entirely focused her attention on what she heard outside.

"I'm Wyatt, and this is Trinity. Doc asked us to run out here and ensure you two got here safely and that you're not starving."

Cameron had no idea who Wyatt and Trinity were, but the mention of Doc made them seem safe enough, so she opened the flap and emerged to stand next to Val.

Under his breath, he said, "You don't listen, ever."

"Welcome to our camp. I'd offer you something to eat, but we only have fish, canned soup, and chili." She pointed to the asparagus. "And that, but I was kind of saving it."

The woman, whose name was Trinity, dismounted the beautiful brown horse. "Then you'll be happy we found you." She opened a saddle bag and pulled out several containers. "Maisey wants her Tupperware back, but word got out you liked her berry pie, so she sent a couple of pieces."

"You brought pie?" Cameron raced toward the pretty blonde and wrapped her in a hug. "You might be my favorite person right this minute."

Val walked over. "I've been tossed aside for pie?"

Wyatt slid from his horse. "Don't worry, man. No one measures up against Maisey's pie." He opened his bags and took out bottled water, instant coffee, canned goods, and a paper bag. "Doc says you might need these."

Val looked inside the bag and grinned. "Now Doc might be my favorite person at this minute." He opened the bag to show Cameron a box of condoms.

"I'm mortified," she said.

Trinity waved that comment away. "Oh, don't worry. He's kind of a father to all of us."

"That's good because I don't have one." She hugged the box of pie to her chest and shook her head. "That's not entirely true. I'm the daughter of donor #381."

Trinity's eyes widened. "That's awesome. I wish I didn't know my father. How lucky that you can make him up."

"Oh, I've been told he's everyone from Clark Gable to Genghis Kahn."

Val's eyes narrowed. "Genghis Kahn?"

She smiled sweetly and turned to him. "That's only when I don't follow the rules."

He laughed. "Which is always." He looked at Wyatt and Trinity before pointing to the rocks and the fire pit. "Would you like to stay a bit?"

Trinity went to the other side of the horse and unpacked more items that she set on the ground. "No, but thank you. We've got plans. It's our day to check the fence." She winked, and Cameron wondered if they were a couple.

"Thanks for the supplies and the visit," Val said.

At their feet was enough food for a few days or more.

"The honey is from Abby. It comes from her hives," Trinity said. "Better than body chocolate." She stuck her boot in the stirrup and lifted to the saddle.

Yep, they had to be a couple, especially since she noticed the smoldering look Wyatt gave Trinity and the way she wiggled in her saddle. She would bet her next year's salary that those two weren't planning on riding the fence but riding each other.

CHAPTER TWENTY-FOUR

Her fishing skills could have bruised Val's ego, but he found it fascinating that side by side, she caught two fish to his one each time they dropped their line into the lake. They'd been camping for several days longer than anticipated, and he knew it was time to return to reality. The biggest problem was he liked who they were together. He completely immersed himself in their fake relationship, and everything seemed real.

He turned to his side and watched her sleep. He loved this quiet time in the morning when she was asleep, and he was free to map out every freckle. She didn't have many, but he'd connected the dots so many times that he could map the exact path from her body to his heart. It was in the little dipper and the single freckle that looked like a heart at the top of her right breast. The pigment change behind her ear resembled a clover—four leaves, of course- because Cameron never did anything part-way.

"You're staring again," she said in that slow morning voice he'd fallen in love with on day one.

"I can't help myself. You mesmerize me."

She pointed to her eyes. "It's these. You might not like me as much if they were blue or green."

"Not true." He'd considered that around day two when he knew his heart was in trouble, but her eye color, while fascinating, wasn't what kept him intrigued. She could find the rainbow in everything. "It's everything about you."

On day four, it rained, and they stayed in the tent eating cold canned chili and playing a game she called never would I ever. It was the most eye-opening experience he'd ever had. She chose to have so little for a woman who could have anything she wanted. It was like she somehow believed all her successes came from the generosity of others. Her agent got her jobs, and her mother guided her. Her fans paid for movies. Not once did she mention her contribution to her success. He didn't see it when he'd watched all her films, but he did now. The directors knew what they had with her and sold it in the millions. She was bottled-up sunshine.

"It's the sex."

After they'd made love the first time, he'd turned their sleeping bag into a large one by zipping them together.

"The sex is amazing, but it's not what makes me love you." There was no doubt in his mind that it was love, and while he wanted to keep her, he knew he couldn't. His day three fantasy had turned into his day six reality. She'd go back to Hollywood, and he'd go back to doing what he'd always done, run the family business.

"You missed your calling. You should have gone into acting. Each time you say those words, I feel them right here." She tapped her heart. "I've grown accustomed to you and how you make me feel. How am I supposed to be the same when I get back to Hollywood."

He leaned over and kissed her. It was a long and slow kiss that said he truly loved her but would have to give her up.

"You'll have actors lining up to play your leading man."

"They have to because they're getting paid. Don't forget I fired you."

He tugged her to his side. "That's right. How could I forget?" He nibbled on her shoulder until she squealed. "Never have I ever been fired before."

"Life is full of firsts. Maybe it will be the turning point to your existence." She rolled back and looked at the top of the tent. "Did you have fun?"

"The best time of my life. I'll take this week and live it in my mind repeatedly."

"Your lips must be tired."

"From kissing you? No way." He wanted to lay there and kiss her forever but knew they had to pack and get back to town.

"No, silly, from smiling too much. Happiness looks good on you."

When they decided to return to the lake house today, he stayed up late, thinking about how good the trip had been for him. The last time he'd felt that free and complete was his hike to the Grand Canyon.

"You look good on me." He rose from the sleeping bag and turned up the lantern.

"Oh my God."

He turned to face her and smiled. "All these days later, and you're still impressed."

She laughed and shook her head. "You have a tick on your ass, and by the size of it, it's been feeding like a king."

He turned to look over his shoulder but couldn't see it. His hand rubbed at his skin until he reached a lump on his left butt cheek. Everything from Lyme disease to infection raced through his head, and panic set in. "Get it off me."

She sat up and turned him around. "Get me the first aid kit."

"Do you know what to do?"

She slapped his right butt cheek. "I played a nurse once in a movie."

"Seriously, I could have Lyme disease."

She tugged on her shirt and stood. "You're in a bit of panic, so let me point out the positives." She nodded to his withering erection. "It's not there."

There was that, but it still didn't solve his problem. "I've got a tick on my ass. There are very few positives."

"I disagree." She rose, stepped out of the tent, and returned seconds later. "You should be grateful that I research everything. It's part of my makeup because I don't want to be ill-prepared." She chewed her lip. "That's not exactly true. When I get this out, you'll want to thank my mother for instilling a thirst for knowledge. My biggest fear was a tick when we decided to go camping." Her shoulders shook. "You should be grateful that bloodsucker is on your behind and not mine. If the situation were reversed, this wouldn't go well for either of us." She pointed to the sleeping bag. "Now lay down and show me that fine rear end of yours."

"Do you know what you're doing?"

She shook her head. "Nope, you're my first patient, but I'd never fished either, and look at how good I am at that."

He couldn't argue, so he did as Cameron told him. "You have to pull it out by the head gently."

"I know what I'm doing." She kneeled beside him and used the hand sanitizer in the first aid box to clean her hands and his bite. She saturated a cotton ball with the stuff and pressed on the tick. "We'll try this first. The article said that sometimes you can use a soapy cotton ball to coax them out."

She counted to thirty and pulled it away. "Nope, I figured as much. It's hard to let go of something so amazing."

Next, she took the tweezers, and he felt a gentle pressure as she tugged the bug from his backside. When she got it free, she held it up for him to see. "Voila. I can now put this on my resume." She rose with the tick and went to the tent flap.

"What are you doing?"

"Helping nature get it right. Something out there wants a meal, and this guy is ready to be sacrificed." She disappeared while he cleaned the bite and dressed.

When she came back inside, he pulled her into his arms. "I really do love you."

She held onto him like he was a lifeline. "I love you too."

He wasn't sure if she was still playing her part, so he repeated it. "No, I mean, I love you."

She stared at him for several seconds. "It's the delirium speaking. We should visit Doc Parker and make sure I got it all out."

He could have told her again, but he believed she knew. She already told him she felt it.

"At least he can treat me for it before I get it."

"Okay, let's pack and get going."

It hurt that they had to leave, and she wasn't fighting to stay, but he reminded himself that her gung-ho spirit was to protect him. It was funny how he'd been hired to do that for her. He should have been in charge of everything, but he'd lost his ability to act rationally when she smiled at him. It wasn't the plane crash that changed everything. It was her. She'd stepped out of her comfort zone to be defiant. He was confident he could make her bend to his will, but in the end, she'd taken charge of his body, mind, and heart.

For a Hollywood type, she wasn't afraid to get her hands dirty. The woman who started breaking down camp wasn't the woman he'd met dressed in stilettos and Chanel. This woman peeled herself off the tarmac, brushed her hair from her face, and moved forward. Cameron Madden was more than she appeared. She was everything.

It took them less than two hours to pack up and return their site back to nature. On the walk back to the car, they were both silent. His came from knowing everything would change when they got back into town.

At the car, he took her pack and placed it in the back of the SUV before walking to her side and opening the door.

"Thank you for everything."

She gave him a weak smile. "I'll never be the same."

He kissed her cheek, and they accomplished everything they set out to do. "You came here to be authentically you. Old Cameron should be incredibly proud of the new you."

She lifted and kissed him gently on the lips. "I'm proud of you."

It was like her to turn her accomplishments around and give credit where it wasn't due. He'd done nothing but basked in her warmth. He felt like a sunflower always turning in her direction. What would happen when her light was no longer a part of his world?

CHAPTER TWENTY-FIVE

At the clinic, Doc looked at her handiwork and declared she'd missed her calling. It was only a tick, but pride filled her through and through. She didn't panic and knew what to do.

"If you ever need a new job, I can put you to work taking care of cuts and scrapes here in the clinic."

"While her nursing skills are commendable, her acting skills are where it's at."

Doc pulled a lifesaver from his pocket and popped it into Val's mouth. "I'm not talking to you, Son. I'm talking to the young miss here." He turned back to Cameron. "You give that some thought."

"I never considered nursing, but I'm touched that you'd think I'd excel at it."

"In my experience, if your heart is in it, you can always make it work. Where's your heart these days, young lady?" He looked from her to Val and back.

Her heart was in that room, internally having a *Notting Hill* moment standing in front of Valery and silently wishing they had a chance at a real life together.

"I love your property. I even caught several fish with an empty hook."

He pointed at Val. "Seems to me that you hooked more than a fish."

The door to the room opened, and a white-haired woman carrying a yellow stenographer's pad entered. "I hate to bother you, but…"

"Come in, Lovey."

The woman looked down at her pad and the pen in her hand.

Cameron recognized that look. "Would you like an autograph?" Most people were afraid to ask, but she felt it was part of the job. It was no different than Doc offering medical advice. It was what he did. She played make-believe and signed autographs.

"There have to be some perks that come with the job." She passed the pad and pen over.

"Who should I make it out to?" She glanced at Doc. "He calls you Lovey, but I assume it's an endearment and not your true name."

"Agatha is my name." She sidled up to Doc and rested her head on his shoulder. "I used to think it was early onset dementia because he never called me Agatha and always called me Lovey, but years later, I know it's because he loves me."

The entire moment touched Cameron. She signed the pad with the following,

To Agatha,

Always choose love,

Cameron Madden

"What about you, young man?" Agatha stared at Val. "Do you have a name for this one?" She nudged Cameron.

"I'm sure he'd call me trouble."

"Not true." Val hopped off the table. "If I had a choice, I'd call you mine."

Doc pointed to the door. "We always have a choice, son." As they walked down the hallway, Doc said, "When you close your eyes and dream, what do you see?"

The question was for Val, but she did what he asked, and when she closed her eyes, all she saw was darkness because a life without Val was like a vast black hole.

"What do I owe you?" Val took his wallet from his pocket.

Doc went behind the counter, pulled out a drawer filled with pharmaceutical samples, and handed him an antibiotic. "This is Aspen Cove. Money is great, but it doesn't buy everything we need." He jutted his chin toward Agatha, who was putting the signed paper in a colorful Colorado frame. "It doesn't buy you love and happiness. That autograph brought my Lovey joy, and that's all we'll accept today." They watched Agatha hang the frame by the cash register. "I think it's time for pie." Doc pointed to the door. "Flip the switch off on your way out." He shuffled toward the stairs. "Let me get my wallet, and I'll be right down, my love. Maisey got the blueberries from Abby, and I'm not missing out."

"Abby, the honey girl?" Cameron asked.

"Makes her sound sweet, right? That girl shot a bear in her house."

"Thank you for sending supplies. We truly appreciate *everything* you sent." She emphasized the word everything, hoping he'd get her meaning. And by the glint in his eyes, he did.

"It's what we do. Aspen Cove takes care of their own."

"But we're just passing through," she said.

"The fact that you landed here makes you kin. I'm glad you enjoyed my land. It's the last piece of my family's legacy

I've got left. It sure would have been nice to turn it over to kin." He winked and shuffled toward the stairs but turned to look over his shoulder. "You know ... my great-grandmother was the only other woman who could fish with an empty hook and feed the masses. Some said the land chose her. What would you say?"

"Could she turn water into wine? That would be a phenomenon."

"Nope, but Zachariah turns mash into moonshine, and it's a miracle he hasn't killed himself."

They walked into the late morning sunshine. Sweetness hung in the air. "Are those muffins I smell?" Val didn't wait for her to answer. He took her hand and led her across the street and into the bakery, where Katie was busy filling up the shelves.

"You're back." She plated up two muffins and set them on the counter. "You better gobble these up before Sahara does." Right then, a little human raced from behind the counter. Her lips were blue. If Cameron didn't see the remnants of berries on the child's face, she would have swept the little one up and raced back to Doc.

"I ate blueberries."

"Really?" Cameron asked. "I'd never know."

Katie rounded the counter with two steaming hot cups of coffee. "I figured you could use a good cup of Joe. It's got to be better than the instant we sent."

Cameron took a seat under the Wishing Wall, and Val moved across from her. "The instant was a step up from lake tea, which was pretty good." Val's kindness still touched her. He'd brought special things for her with limited space, like s'mores and tea. She couldn't recall a single time when a date went out of their way for her. Most of her dates expected her to do for them since she made a lot of money. In that way, Doc was right. Money was great, but it didn't buy important things.

"You got your wish," Katie said to Val.

"It was a dream come true." He took a bite of the muffin. "This is pretty great too."

Katie picked her little girl up. "This is my dream. Aspen Cove made it all happen. Everything good about my life came from here. Including those blueberries."

"Abbie's?" Cameron asked.

"She got a bumper crop this year and shared. It's not blueberry day, but you take it when the universe gives you a gift." She glanced at the Wishing Wall. "Are you still waiting for your wish to come true, or did that happen already?"

Thankfully, the door opened, and in walked a customer, so she didn't have to answer. What she wanted was the role of a lifetime. Katie once asked what that looked like, and she always thought it was a coveted part, but now she wasn't sure.

They finished their muffins and coffee and left money on the counter to pay before returning to the lake house. On the porch was a package. She recognized the envelope, the thickness, and the return address. It was a manuscript. She'd told Lucifer to find her something good and knew he had.

"Oh, my goodness. Lucifer found me a part." She hugged the parcel to her chest and heard Katie's warning. *Be careful what you ask for.*

CHAPTER TWENTY-SIX

She entered the living room and flopped onto the couch, placing the envelope next to her.

Val went to the kitchen and took a bottle of wine from the rack. This was a celebration. He poured two glasses and joined her. "Are you going to open it?"

"It's a little early for wine."

"Never too early to celebrate."

She took the glass and sipped the dry red wine before setting it on the nearby table. "I'm afraid. What if it's not everything I wanted?"

"But what if it is? What if it's everything you've ever dreamed about?" He sat on the couch. The only thing separating them was what was in that envelope. His brain screamed, "*Liar!*" There was so much separating them. They left their tent and came back to reality. While reality never lived up to his dreams, he used to be comfortable with it. Maybe comfortable was the wrong word. He'd accepted his lot in life. Then Cameron appeared and showed him something different—something extraordinary and magical. His reality wasn't all that enticing, but hers was looking up, and he'd support her.

"You're right." She lifted the envelope and stared at it. "There better be a good role in here. I told him not to send me anything unless it was different and new."

"You'll never find out until you open it."

She held it so tightly in her hands that her knuckles turned white. "But what if it's just more of the same?"

He knew what more of the same felt like. It was slogging through mud, knee-deep in an endless bog. "Then you say no, and nothing has changed."

She hugged the envelope to her chest. "But everything changes because it's like a message from Lucky telling me I'm incapable of more."

He scooted closer to get her full attention. "You can be anything you want. As Doc said, you always have a choice." That had resonated with him since Doc had said the words, but were they true for everyone? Were some lives driven by the individual, or did everyone have a choice? If the latter was true, was it right to choose something that affected so many? Did his happiness usurp his father's dreams? What about his dreams—did they count?

"You're right."

She smiled and tore the tab that opened the envelope. Her fingers shook as she took out the thick document. She skimmed the cover page and pulled it free to show him.

Cameron,

You asked for something different. I delivered. Your dreams are about to come true. Please read it and call me. I need an answer soon.

Lucky

Val picked up his wine. "It's five o'clock somewhere. Shall we toast to your dreams coming true?"

She took her wine glass and touched his. "What about your dreams?"

"I got to camp with a beautiful woman who made all my dreams come true. I got my wish. It's your turn."

She laid her hand over the manuscript and let her fingers reverently skim the title. "*Breakfast with Tiffany*." She scanned the front page. "It's based on *Breakfast at Tiffany's*."

"Is that good?"

"They want me to be the next Audrey Hepburn."

"I've never seen the original. It sounds light and airy."

"She's an escort." Cameron turned the page.

"Oh, that is a departure." He'd made love to her, and she had all the skills to play an escort, but the thought made him want to tear that script from her hands and toss it aside. He didn't want any man thinking about her in the way he had experienced first-hand. "Is that what you want?"

"It could be career suicide. I'm no Audrey Hepburn."

"No, but you could be the next Audrey."

She smiled and sipped her wine. "I'm a little old."

"You're only thirty-five."

She took her hand off the manuscript and slugged him. He was glad to see her knuckles were no longer sore from hitting the last asshole.

"You know I'm only thirty-two, but that's near ancient in Hollywood."

"Modeling maybe, but not acting. Look at Sandra Bullock, Viola Davis, Salma Hayek, and Lucy Liu—all women older than you and still rocking it." He rose from the couch. "I imagine you'll want to read your blockbuster hit."

She looked up at him with gratitude shining in her eyes. "Do you mind?"

His heart ached, but how could he mind? "No, I need to check in with my family. I'm sure a new assignment needs my attention or at least research." He took his glass of wine and walked outside.

The first call he made was to his mother.

"Valery, where have you been?"

"Camping?" Even the word made him smile, but the memories made his heart take off like the bullet out of Georgio's gun, only the end of the trip hurt worse.

"Aren't you working?"

"Sort of. My client fired me and made it her mission to make me smile."

"Who is this woman? Do I know her? And if not, would I like her?"

He chewed on the first question silently for several seconds. Cameron was everything. "You don't know her personally. She's an actress."

"Oh, one of those." His mother had a distaste for the rich and famous. The family had served them all their lives, and his mother always felt they took more than they gave. Her family was never home but on someone else's turf taking care of someone else's business.

"No, Mom, she's different. You'd like her."

He waited for what seemed like a lifetime for her to respond. "Different from Monica? I never liked that woman. She was a taker, not a giver. Did you say camping?"

He walked down the stairs and toward the water. "Yes, and she caught fish with no bait."

"Sounds like she hooked you too, my boy."

He wasn't sure if he should be honest. He hadn't been completely honest with himself yet, but he always tried to be open and never lied to his mother. "She did, but it's not meant to be. She's got her career, and I've got you guys."

Silence followed.

"Mom? Are you there?"

She cleared her throat. "Valery, when your father told you to keep it together, I don't think he meant you were supposed to sacrifice your life."

"Family isn't a sacrifice." Deep in his heart, he knew that wasn't always the truth. Life tugged him in many directions, but the hardest pulls always brought him from what he wanted to do to where he needed to be.

"Family isn't always an upward and lateral extension. What about making a family for yourself? I had dreams, and they had nothing to do with Vortex. You are all married to this damn company, and my dreams aren't coming true. Where are my grandchildren? Do you think keeping it together meant stopping the family line? That's not what your father wanted. He meant to help your family heal, move on, and create your future. You've done a great job keeping us together, but we were never going to fall apart. We're family, and we'll always have each other's backs. I love you, my boy, but I don't need you to be the man of my family. Isn't it time you forged your path?"

Until he met Cameron, he'd thought he was on his path, but the key was he hadn't chosen it.

"I'm going to think about that, Mom. Thank you for your wisdom."

"You don't have to follow my advice, but I'm your momma, and you should listen. You'll never be too old to turn over my knee."

He chuckled. "Yes, ma'am. You've given me a lot to consider."

"Is that girl still with you?"

"She's here, but she's not with me. She's got a new opportunity that will change her life."

"Her best opportunity sounds like you."

"Says my mother. Talk to you soon, okay?" They hung up, and he walked the shoreline for over an hour, and when he turned around, he saw the big bull elk standing in his path. They stared at each other for several seconds. It was like the animal was strengthening the message for Val to make his path as the giant beast fearlessly walked into the water.

He knew if he and Cameron were to forge a path together, they would have to leave their old identities behind. What worked for them at the lake was that out there, they had no one to please but each other, and they were good at it.

Determined to go after his dream, he walked into the house and heard her speaking on the phone.

"Lucky, oh my God. You did it. I've only read half, but it's everything I always wanted."

His heart slid from his chest to his throat, and then free fell to the ground.

Cameron gasped. "I have to be there in two days?" She noticed he was standing there, and he could see that she was torn. He could see clearly now that she loved him, and he loved her more than he could ever have imagined would be possible, which is why he wouldn't make her choose.

He smiled and said, "I'll make the arrangements."

He didn't want to fly, but it was the quickest way back, so he walked into the kitchen, called the travel service for Vortex, and planned their return trip to Hollywood. This time they were flying commercial. He'd rather protect her from an adoring crowd than a plane malfunction where he had zero control. Those were less likely on a national airline—at least, that was his hope.

He was writing down the final plan when she entered the kitchen and wrapped her arms around his waist. "Are you okay with this?"

He turned to look into her eyes—eyes that could jump-start his heart as well as crush it. "It's what you have to do."

"But what about us?"

He kissed her forehead and told his very first lie wrapped in the truth. "We only exist here. In the real world, we'd never make it. I'd be gone, and you'd be busy. In the real world, we live to work and not work to live." He hugged her tight and stepped back. "This was a real-life blockbuster. How often do people get that?" He moved into the living room, picking up his things. "You should pack. Our plane leaves tomorrow afternoon from Denver."

"Plane?"

He stopped and stared at her. "It's the quickest route."

"Are you coming with me?" Her jaw dropped.

"You hired me to protect you."

"But I fired you."

"I'll always protect you." He was doing that right now by taking her back to her real life. She could never belong to him if she belonged to the world.

CHAPTER TWENTY-SEVEN

Leaving Aspen Cove felt wrong, but what was a woman with a plan to do? She'd gotten what she asked for, and it seemed wrong to test fate. She wanted the most significant role of her life, and FedEx delivered it to her door.

"Do we have everything we need?" she asked.

"Yep." Val put the last of the borrowed camping supplies in the back of the SUV and closed the back. "Bowie said he'd get everything back to the owners. I figured you could hand-deliver Maisey's Tupperware since we have to eat."

He handed her the old-school container with an olive-green snap-on cover. She glanced back at the house. They hadn't been there long, but she'd enjoyed their time together. "Did you ever see the elk again?" It saddened her that she wouldn't have the opportunity to see such a majestic creature once more.

"Yes," he said. "He crossed my path last night. It was like he came to say farewell. It was just him. The harem was nowhere in sight."

Her heart lurched. "Do you think they chose another mate and abandoned him?" That's what it felt like for her right then. She had a choice, and she chose her career. Or did she? It wasn't like Val asked her to stay. He only confirmed that they didn't have a future together. Something told her that if he'd asked, she would have stayed, but she'd always wonder.

"I can't say, but he looked at peace with whatever happened. Sometimes you have to go with what life throws at you." He walked around to open her door. "I'll take another look around and lock up." She climbed into the passenger seat as he walked away.

Since last night, Val had been back to his grumpy self. His conversations were short and professional. Her paramour had left, and the unemotional protector was back. She'd hoped that on their last night, he'd come to her bed and make love to her as he had at the lake, but he didn't. She probably should have been grateful, but it emptied her.

The driver's door opened, and he took his seat. "I'll drop off the supplies if you want to get us a table in the diner." He drove away from the house and dropped her in front of Maisey's.

She walked inside to find most of the tables full, with one next to Doc and Agatha free, so she took it.

"I hear you're leaving," Agatha said as she neared.

"News travels fast." Cameron took a seat facing the door.

Doc laid down his paper. "Faster than a pandemic but generally more pleasant," Doc said. "Except this news. It would have been nice to keep you around."

"I got what I came here for."

"Did you?" Agatha asked.

"What did you come here for?" Doc folded his paper and set it aside.

"Perspective."

Maisey rushed over. "I'll give you some perspective. It's as busy as beads and boobs at Mardi Gras. If you take what I give you, you'll eat more quickly. If not, order at your peril because Ben's temper is hotter than today's grill. He wanted an easy Monday, and he got a misplaced payday Friday."

"Mystery meal it is." She held up two fingers. "Val is on his way."

"Coming right up." Maisey overturned two coffee mugs and filled them to the rim before her white loafers squeaked across the checkerboard floor.

Val walked in and took the seat across from Cameron. "What did I miss?"

Cameron laughed. "Nothing and everything. It's mystery meal or nothing, and Doc was asking about perspective."

Doc shook his head. "Nope, Cameron said she came here to get some, and her work is done."

Val doctored her coffee the way she liked it and kept his black. He was exactly what you saw while she was complicated.

"Her work is just beginning. She's got the opportunity of a lifetime."

Doc picked up his mug and sipped. "Life is full of opportunities. How does one know which is the right one to chase?"

"It's impossible to know, so it's important to keep chasing them. Opportunities, choices, dreams, aren't they the same?" Val asked. "If you don't seek it, you'll never get it."

She listened to them debate the benefits of opportunity and the risks of not taking chances.

"But what if your perspective is skewed and you make the wrong choice?" she asked.

Doc smiled. "We always have choices. It's like driving down the highway and coming to a fork. You may turn left when you should have turned right, but you have a choice. See where the path leads. You can always retrace your steps and go the other way if it's not someplace you want to be. The path you chose isn't a dead end. It's merely one way to travel."

His words sat comfortably inside her. Why did life have to be all or nothing? Wasn't the journey half the fun? She'd spent her life moving at a breakneck pace to get to a destination, but she never enjoyed the voyage. That was perspective.

Maisey dropped off two plates piled high with pancakes, eggs, and sausage. "Enjoy and come back again soon. I was hoping you'd stay. I like the good tippers."

The door opened, and Red walked in. He looked toward her and Val and shook his head. It seemed like he'd turn and walk out, but he didn't. He approached.

"Hey, I heard you two were leaving." He shoved his hands in his pockets and looked at the ground. "I wanted to apologize for being a shit. I'm not a bad person. I'm just a man who lets the wrong head think."

Val stood, and Cameron was sure Red would be eating a five-finger sandwich soon, but that didn't happen. Val patted Red on the back. "That's the manliest thing I've heard you say since I met you. Admitting a problem is half the cure." Val took his seat, and Cameron let out a held breath.

"You two are perfect for each other. Even I can see that."

Val dug into his pancakes. "I agree, but we're on different paths. I'm turning right, and she's turning left." He smiled at her. "But according to Doc, someday, we may cross paths again, and maybe by then, our perspectives will have changed. Maybe someday we'll want the same scenic route. Maybe someday, it will be our time."

Red leaned in and kissed the top of her head. "I wish the best for you always." He turned and went to a booth on the other side of the room and joined the two women from the other night. Some things would change, but Red wasn't one of them.

They dined quickly and headed to Denver. Panic set in as soon as they got on the plane, and it didn't leave until they landed safely in Los Angeles. The fact that they didn't crash meant all signs for a positive outcome were pointing in the right direction as they pulled up to her building. Val helped her to the penthouse entrance and set her bags outside the door. He didn't walk out of the elevator but stood with one foot in and one foot out.

"Don't forget me," she said.

He smiled and stepped back. "You're unforgettable." When the elevator door closed, she looked around and found the once-bright house, filled with white, gold, and light, darkened. Nothing would be the same. She knew that now, but it wasn't what she had left for. She'd gone for a change, and she got it. This was her new path. Where would it lead her?

CHAPTER TWENTY-EIGHT

The hardest thing he ever did was take that elevator down to the first floor and walk out of the building. It struck him funny how perspective worked. Not too long ago, he was happy to walk past the waterfall, climb into the SUV, and drive away. He might have even considered himself ecstatic that she might take longer than ten minutes to show up, and he could leave without a lick of guilt eating at him.

As he passed Gary, all he felt was regret. Not that he'd fallen in love with her—that was the biggest surprise of all—but that he felt everything so painfully. It gave him pause to wonder if he'd flipped a switch all those years ago in an attempt to survive.

"Does she need anything?" Gary asked.

"Not that I know of, but I'm sure she'll let you know. She seems to be completely focused on the future." It wasn't often that he saw his clients grow, but he'd watch Cameron bloom at that lake. He was pretty sure it was time, space, and opportunity colliding, but he was grateful to see the transformation even though he was sure he had nothing to do with it. Most of the time, he watched his clients misbehave. This time Cameron blessed him with growth, and he liked that.

"She's one of the nicest people I know," Gary said.

"She *is* the nicest person I know." Val shook Gary's hand and walked into the sunshine. Somehow it didn't seem as bright or warm without Cameron by his side. He glanced at his watch and figured he had enough time to drop off the car and catch his flight home. Not his home, but the home base for the business in New York—his mother's house.

He phoned his mother and told her he'd be there late that night. She mentioned something about his siblings all coming over for breakfast. It sounded more like an inquisition or intervention than a family meeting, but he couldn't be bothered with the details.

PER HIS PRE-CAMERON SCHEDULE, he was up at five with a cup of coffee and the company ledgers. His mother's home sat on Oyster Bay overlooking Centre Island. It wasn't the brownstone he'd grown up in, sharing three spare bedrooms with six kids. This was his father's dream for his mother—coffee on the veranda surrounded by blooming colorful hydrangea in pinks, purples, blues, and white. Blankets of pachysandra filled the neatly trimmed flowerbed to add the green necessary for nature. It was beautiful, but it wasn't him. He was pine trees and shrubs and wildflowers that sprouted and grew through the rugged terrain. He was cans of open-fire chili, hooting owls and wild elk greeting him.

He shoved the spreadsheet in a nearby folder and leaned back to close his eyes and remember the blissful moments. Still, all that ever showed up in his mind's eye was Cameron pulling in a fish on an empty hook or that serious look she gave him when she held that tick in the tweezers and told him she was helping the food chain.

"What's that smile for?" His mother had snuck up on him. He was definitely off his game. At work, an unprotected moment could be dangerous, but his mother wasn't a threat.

"Thinking about bugs and beasts."

She took a seat across from him. "And that makes you smile."

"It's all perspective."

"It is, and I've been thinking a lot about it lately." She sipped her coffee and stared at the water. "This was the dream. Sitting outside with family and enjoying the fruits of our labor, but sometimes the dreams don't always mesh with reality."

He knew his mom was getting at something, but her process was different from his, and she'd get to where she needed to be in her time.

"Is there something you wanted to talk about?"

She shook her head. "No, but I owe you an apology for the other day. I went on about my dreams and spent very little time discussing yours."

He kicked out his feet. If his instincts were right, he had a few minutes before his family would all converge, and this peaceful interaction would take on a different vibe.

"I've never been a dreamer."

"Not true. You dreamed a lot when you were a kid." She smiled. "You would be a pirate, a mobster, a movie star, and a hiker. You wanted to climb mountains and jump out of planes, and lately, all you seem to be doing is falling from them." She waved her hand through the air. "This place is a dream, but it would be a nightmare for me if my children's aspirations were buried because they thought this was their vision."

The door opened, and three of his six siblings walked in, led by Viv, who was dressed in jeans and a T-shirt like it was a day off. Odin and Torren were right behind her, both suited up like they were heading to Wall Street. Both probably were since they'd taken on security jobs for high-end hedge fund traders this month.

"The others just parked," Odin said as he took the seat next to his mother.

Moments later, in walked Ramsey, Easton, and Xander. They all had a worried, desperate look to them that brought him back to the day they sat around the large dining table of the old brownstone to decide the fate of the family after their father passed. Val didn't regret one decision he'd made that day. He'd stepped up, and because he did, they were all okay. He'd ruled his family with the same directness his father had.

"Is this an intervention?" he asked as they gathered around the large outdoor table. His mother's staff brought out trays of fruit and croissants with various jams and spreads and set them on the table along with coffee and mugs.

"Do you need one?" Ramsey asked.

"I don't think so, but you tell me." Of his brothers, Ramsey was more like him. He was direct and didn't like the useless-ness of endless conversation. He had a mission and got it done. Outside of Val, he was the one that billed the most because he was always on the move. Part of him wondered if that was because he was still looking for something. Val thought it was just the way he worked until he was able to spend downtime with Cameron and realized he didn't need the constant shuffle of schedules to fill his life. All he needed was the right person to fill his life, but, in all things, sacrifices had to be made, and he was often the one to make them. He'd done it for his family, and he'd do it for her. Sometimes, bad luck was simply bad timing.

His mother stood and tapped a glass. "I've called this meeting because it's time for a reorganization."

His mother owned Vortex and was the head of the company. They were all officers, but no one would usurp her power and control. She'd given birth to the crew and had signed the first page, then incorporated Vortex Security Services. She had the final say in the beginning, and so it would be at the end whenever that came.

She cleared her throat. "I will never force you out, but I will give you an out."

Viv rubbed her face. "Sounds like an intervention." She turned to Val. "What the hell did you do?"

"Me? I didn't do anything."

"He crashed another plane," Torren said. "You seem to be doing that a lot lately."

Val's nerves bristled. "I wasn't flying it. It's been a bit of bad luck."

His mother cleared her throat. "This isn't one of those math situations when you add up two negatives and get a positive. I think it's time to cut our losses."

He stared at his family. "I'm at a loss."

His mother walked around the table until she was behind him. "No, you've been an asset, but you can't be one if you're dead, and lately, this business hasn't been kind to you." She squeezed his shoulders and skimmed her hands over the backs of his siblings as she walked by them in what looked like a duck, duck, goose game, but she took a seat before anyone was tagged and had to run.

He felt like somehow, he was out of the game before it began. "What are you getting at?"

Odin set his hands on the table, but the force of the hit made it vibrate. "It's time, brother. Time for you to step aside."

Val's heart seized in his chest. "You're firing me?"

Viv placed her hand on his. "No, big brother, we're setting you free. You've raised us and this business. It's our gift." She smiled. "A little bird whispered that there's someone who could make you smile. I'd like to see that."

"I'm not leaving the company. This is what I do." His skin prickled with what felt like anger, but there was something else mixed with it. It was an adrenaline rush. Like somehow, his tether had broken free, but he didn't know which way to run. He was like a dog uncaged, and while he liked the idea of freedom, he didn't know what to do with it.

"You will always be part of the board. Always be a paid employee, but you've served your time. If you stay at the head of the company, there's no room for growth," Vivian said.

"You want to run the company, Viv?" He'd never thought about what he at the helm meant for the others.

"Yes, it makes sense. I'm the only other V in the family."

He took a few calming breaths and stared at his brothers, who didn't seem bothered by Vivian jumping the ranks. "What about all of you? Is this the life you want?"

"It's what we know for now."

That made sense to him. Everyone was on their path. Everyone but him. "Is this what you want? You want me gone?" It should have hurt, but it didn't. He'd seen the writing on the wall. He was a cog in a well-oiled machine. But so were his siblings; he knew if they removed his piece, they'd all fall in line and fill in the space he left behind by his absence.

"It's not that we want you gone," Easton said. "We just want you happy." He shrugged. "I'm with Viv, and I don't think I've ever seen that."

Vivian pulled a folder out of her bag and pulled out a contract. "It's a leave of absence form. You're on paid leave to find bliss for the next six months. I'd say it's a win-win situation. You can explore and see what or who else is out there or come back if you want."

"You're giving me an open agreement to come and go."

Xander held up his hand. "Nope. You have to go and not come back for six months first. Where will you start your journey?"

His mother smiled. "Maybe Hollywood?"

He saw where her sights were. She was an Armstrong and wouldn't stop manipulating us to get what she wanted; right now, she wanted grandchildren.

"Sorry to dash your hopes, Mom, but my client is back to her life."

His mom's sweet smile grew into a grin. "For now. But I know my son, and he'll figure it out. He took a business way too young and turned it into something wonderful. Certainly, he could win the heart of the woman he wants."

"Let's hope she picks better men than movies. Watching one is like eating a gallon of ice cream with every known candy sprinkle added."

He'd thought the same thing when he'd watched them. "They grow on you."

"Is it settled then? You'll take some time off? At least to get out of your plane crash mode, and we do what we do best?" Viv asked.

"What's that, Viv?" He poured himself a fresh cup of coffee and sat back.

"Looking after those we love."

He picked up the pen and scribbled his name on the bottom of the contract, which gave him everything and gave them nothing but peace of mind. Somehow it was enough for his family to love him. He was like them. He'd let Cameron go because he knew this journey of self-discovery had to be traveled on her own. She was stepping out of her comfort zone, and the only way to succeed was to do it alone, but he'd be waiting on the other side if she got there and wanted the same things as he did.

As he shoved the contract aside, his phone buzzed. When he looked down, he smiled.

It was a message from Cameron. "Things will get busy soon, but I want you to know there won't be a day I won't miss you."

CHAPTER TWENTY-NINE

Three months into filming *Breakfast With Tiffany*, Cameron both hated and loved the experience. It was refreshing to stretch her wings, but she played the same girl in the end. She was sparkly, goofy, and sunshine, only this time, she had quirks and a better leading actor.

"We need to reshoot the last love scene," the director said.

"What was wrong with it?" She'd never in her life questioned anything, but lately, she'd been questioning everything. It wasn't coming from a place of disrespect but a place of knowing. Those love scenes were the best she'd ever filmed. She knew it in her heart because each time she kissed Matthew Michelson, in her head she was kissing Val, and nothing had ever been more perfect than when she made love to Val. Sex could be just sex but making love was something entirely different. And while she and Matthew never did the actual deed, she used all the emotions she'd found in that tent in the Rockies to pull out her best performances.

"Nothing on your part. Matt's pace is off, making it look clumsy and awkward."

She nearly choked upon hearing those words. The

thought that her leading man could look awkward in anything was beyond her. Those were generally words used to describe her, but she'd gotten nothing short of accolades since they started filming.

She shook herself from her head to her toes. "Okay, I'll be ready in ten." Not long ago, she would have said she was ready then, but she realized it took time to transition, and that's what she'd been doing for the last few months. She'd moved from being her mother's daughter and Lucky's client to Val's paramour and more. She had gotten the role of a lifetime, but it didn't feel nearly as important as the one that came before it. The one where she found herself drinking lake tea by a campfire with a man who was inherently grouchy but made her heart sing. He'd made her fall in love with him, or maybe that part was inevitable. They were both looking for something, and they found it in the arms of each other, but the timing was terrible. He'd abandoned her on her doorstep and never looked back.

At the time, that didn't seem kind, but she saw it differently as she had grown over the last several months. He loved her in the best way he knew how. He gave her the time she needed to love herself. That was the problem all along. She'd never trusted her gut, and as the time neared to wrap up the picture, her soul was screaming at her to be happy.

She called her mom with five minutes left until she needed to be back on set.

"I hear you're killing it."

Cameron smiled. Her life had changed. Where her mother once offered advice, she now offered praise each time she got on the phone.

"It's been good. I have to reshoot a sex scene, and then I think we've got about a week or so before we wrap up."

"Wow, that's ahead of schedule. You're a director's dream."

She walked into her trailer, where her assistant was laying out the lingerie she was supposed to wear—silk pajamas with pictures of pine trees and owls.

"I only have a few minutes. I'm at a crossroads, but I want to know what you consider to be the best decision of your life?"

"Are you unhappy?" her mother asked. "I can still kick ass if anyone bothers my little girl."

Cameron let her robe fall and put on the soft silk. It didn't feel as lovely as the shirt she'd snagged that first night from Val. "I'm not unhappy. My life is good, but I feel it could be better. When was the first time you were truly happy?"

She expected the silence to drag on, but it didn't. "It was the day I had you."

"Really?" She expected her mother to talk about the awards, dresses, or parts, but the answer surprised her. "Why would you say that?"

"Because it's important to speak the truth to ourselves. My Oscar-winning moment was the day I had you. Look, you weren't perfect, but neither was I. Alone we are simply people, but together we are a force to reckon with. What we bring to the real-life screen of our lives is authenticity. Without it, there's nothing genuine. Often it takes the right person to make you want more for yourself. What do you want?"

"I want it all."

"Then go after it, baby."

She hung up with her mother and walked onto the set to refilm the sex scene. It would be the last time she'd have to act with Matthew, but in her head, when she closed her eyes, it was always the first time with Val.

When the scene was complete, she rushed into her trailer. With press junkets starting, she'd need a security team, and she knew just the man for the job.

Her newfound sense of strength and courage left her as she hovered over the last digit of Vortex Security's number. Why was she so nervous to reach out to them? Maybe it was because she was afraid of rejection. She pressed the button anyway because fear never moved you truly forward.

"Vortex Security, this is Vivian Armstrong. How can I help you?"

Cameron cleared her throat. "Hello, this is Cameron Madden. I'm a former client." She hadn't considered that they wouldn't take her back. She was probably one of the only people who'd fired them in the past.

"Ms. Madden. How are you?"

"Umm, I'm good. I'm wrapping up a project and thought it would be good to hire security for the upcoming launch."

There was a moment of silence. "Normally, this is handled by your agent."

"Yes, but ... I have a special request."

In the background, Cameron heard the click of nails on keys. "I can offer you Xander, as early as next month."

Her heart sank. "I was hoping for Valery?"

"Oh. He's on an extended leave of absence."

Cameron's heart clacked shut like the director's hand snapping the clapboard closed. "Is he okay?"

"He's great, or I think he is. I really don't know."

"Well, is he, or isn't he?" She rarely lost her patience. It wasn't part of her persona, but when it came to Val, this was news she needed to know. They'd exchanged a few hellos, but each time they did, it made the longing for him that much harder, so their messages grew longer between until they stopped altogether a few weeks ago.

"Let me put you on hold."

"No!" she yelled, but Vivian had already done so, and music played in the background.

Moments later, the line picked up. "Transferring to Vivian."

"But I thought I was speaking to—"

"Is this Cameron?" an older woman's voice asked. "Colorado Cameron?"

"Yes."

"This is Val's mother. If you want to see him happy, go back to the last place you knew him to be so." The phone went dead, and Cameron stared at her cell for seconds past the hang-up.

Did that mean Val wasn't happy? Where was his happy place? She only knew of two locations. One was the Grand Canyon, and she'd never find him there, but the other was Aspen Cove, and if that's where he was, that's where she knew she should be.

———

IT TOOK two more weeks to wrap up the movie. She could have jumped a plane and headed for Colorado, but it was never wise to rush the important things—love being the most important.

On a Friday morning, she had Gary pack up her SUV, and she headed out by car. Since that first journey, she'd gotten her driver's license, bought a car, and found the exact pair of banana pants Val had worn on their first day together. If they were going to start forever, it should be in those pants.

She stopped at her mother's the first night, and they held each other while they talked about love, life, and longing. And it was decided right then that a lovely life shouldn't be lived with longing. That's when her mom broke the news that she and Lucky would be marrying, and he would be Cameron's father after all. He wasn't her birth father but was the only person her mother had ever truly loved besides Cameron. They'd set aside their desires long ago only to discover that some dreams, like riches and careers, fell flat when it came to things of the heart.

When she set out the next day on the final journey to her heart's desire, she rushed toward Aspen Cove with wild abandon. She didn't stop at Doc's or the diner, but at the bakery, where she found Katie cleaning up for the day.

"Look what the cat dragged in." Katie wiped her hands on her apron and rushed around the counter to squeeze Cameron. "You look almost as good as a turtle brownie. Only almost because … you know … there's caramel."

"You're a sight for sore eyes." She hadn't realized how much she'd missed this place until now. It wasn't like she'd spent much time in town, but the time she did was memorable. Katie was the type of woman you met once and knew all your life. She was sweet tea and hospitality. "How did that wish come out?" She pointed to The Wishing Wall.

"You were right. I needed to be careful what I wished for."

Katie's shoulders sagged. "Not so great, huh?"

She didn't want her friend to think she'd failed, so she shook her head. "No, it was everything I thought I wanted, but I'm selfish and want more."

"There's nothing wrong with being selfish from time to time." Katie tore off a sticky note and handed it to Cameron. "There isn't a limit to wishes." Katie picked up a pen from the table and placed it in Cameron's hand. "Do you want a muffin while you're wishing?"

"I'll take a collection of sweets. If things go the way I plan,

I'll be sharing; if not, I'll be burying my sorrows in them." She wrote her wish on the note and stuck it to the wall. All it said was, *With him, all things are possible*. Many would believe it was a religious reference, but this was all about Val because only with him was everything achievable

Katie set the box of goodies on the counter. "If you're looking for a certain mountain man, rumor has it he's been up at the lake."

Cameron gave her a confused look. "Doc's lake or the big lake by Frank's house?"

"I think you know. It's the only lake that means something to both of you."

Joy raced through Cameron like a sparrow after a bug. "I've got to go." She placed far too much money on the counter for what she'd bought, but she was sure she owed Katie a lot more than she'd ever paid.

"He isn't going anywhere, honey. He's been waiting for you."

Tears brimmed in Cameron's eyes. "I'm worth waiting for."

"That's what I hear."

Cameron hugged the box closely to her chest when she ran from the bakery to climb into her SUV and head for home. She didn't care if it was a tent or a sleeping bag on the ground. Val was home. How funny was it that she once thought Valery was not the man of her dreams when he was the only man who could make them come true.

CHAPTER THIRTY

Val waited anxiously for any sign of life coming from the highway. He'd grown up in the city and spent most of his life in the hustle and bustle, but there was something to be said for small-town living.

News traveled like the wind in Aspen Cove. As soon as Cameron's bumper crossed the town line, Aiden Cooper called to tell him she was back. The subsequent notification came minutes ago from Katie, who informed him that there was a delivery on the way. That's when he said goodbye to Wes Covington and the Cooper brothers and walked down the new driveway to where he knew Cameron would land.

The ink hadn't even dried on the contract before he phoned Doc Parker and made an offer on the land. The property was a good investment; even if Cameron had never shown up, he wouldn't have regretted the purchase. Buying a piece of the mountains guaranteed his soul a place to live forever.

Leaning against a tree, he watched a dark SUV wind through the tree line on its way to him. He had a sense of pride for having taught her how to drive. He erased that thought immediately and let out a snort. He hadn't taught her anything. He'd only allowed her to try something new in an environment where she'd felt safe. That's how it had been with them. They had become each other's soft place to land.

The tires crunched on gravel and pine needles as she came to a stop along the edge of the property. The landscape looked different than it had the last time they were there. He'd built a road and fenced in the property, but nothing was visible from where she'd parked the car, and he could see the confusion in her expression. It was like she knew she was on the right path, but maybe had taken a wrong turn. She had an actor's face with a thousand emotions, but the only one he saw now was puzzlement. Was she at the right place or not?

She opened the door and got out, and it took everything he had inside him not to rush over and sweep her into his arms. He wanted to but didn't because moments like this should be relished. Finding Cameron dressed in blue jeans and a sunshine T-shirt wasn't his norm. The last time he'd seen her was this week on Entertainment Tonight plugging the new movie. She was wearing one of those fancy outfits that showed off far too much leg and cleavage for his inner elk to find comfort. But today was different. Today she wore a familiar T-shirt. He thought it was the one from the Four Seasons, but as he zoomed his attention to the graphic on the front, he noticed it didn't say I Chose Santa Fe, but read, I Choose You.

He made a noise, and she jumped into the air. Her hand went straight to her purse, pulling out something and holding it up high. "I've got bear spray." She pressed a pump, and the smell of lilacs filled the air.

"I'd say that's an attractor, sweetheart." He came out of

the shadows with a grin on his face. "If you're trying to scare me away, you're using the wrong technique." That perfume brought out the primal side in him.

She stopped short and looked into the brush as if trying to find his voice.

He broke free from the edge to see her more clearly. "It's about time you showed up. I've been waiting forever."

"Oh, Val." She took off toward him at a sprint and didn't stop until she was in his arms. "You disappeared." Her lips crushed against his until it was hard to tell where he ended, and she began. With her legs wrapped around his waist, he carried her down the path toward their future.

"No honey, I'm here. I've been here the whole time." He nipped and bit at her lips while his hands cupped the round of her bottom.

"You could have told me. I would have come."

He marched her toward the lake, all the while kissing her and rememorizing the feel of her in his arms.

"Don't you understand? This is our journey. This is where we began. The fact that we ended back here means something." He covered her mouth and kissed her until his lungs were practically bursting from lack of air.

She laughed. "It means I have decent driving and GPS skills."

He moved down the newly laid road until it opened to a clearing by the lake. "No, your heart was programmed to the same coordinates as mine."

As he entered the clearing, he reluctantly placed her on her feet. The cabin was nearly built. He'd taken a chance by making something he wasn't sure she'd want, but she'd been very clear about her needs. She didn't want a mansion. She wanted a small cabin big enough to house them and their two kids.

"What did you do?"

He walked her toward the front door of the small two-story structure. It wasn't a fancy house but a cabin kit that went up in no time and allowed custom features. They could live off the grid by solar power if they chose but had the amenities necessary for a posh existence.

"The last time I was here, I did a little method acting."

Her fingers brushed the edge of the rocking chair on the porch. In the morning, he'd come out with a cup of coffee and watch the breeze ripple across the lake. Every once in a while, he'd glimpse an elk on the other side and wonder if it was the same one from Cove Lake.

"If I recall, you were very good at it."

"No, that's the thing. I wasn't good at it. I don't know how to pretend with you." He cupped her cheek. "The thing is, I left you because it was the right thing to do, but it wasn't the easiest thing to do."

"It sucked, but I understand why you did it." She walked to the rail and leaned over, looking toward the lake.

The setting sun caught the gold in her hair. She was angelic. "A path you don't forge on your own can't be trusted."

"You knew I'd come back." She turned in a circle. "You built this because of me."

He shook his head, "No, I built this for us. I figured if it worked for Kevin Costner, then I had a chance."

She flung herself into his arms. "If you build it, they will come."

"The only person I wanted to show up was you."

"I'm here, Val, and I'm not leaving."

He'd waited long enough for happiness and refused to wait another second. In a single motion, he swept her into his arms and carried her over the threshold of their dreams.

Today was the first day of their new forever. A life they'd carved out through years of sacrifice and commitment.

People said good things came to those who waited, but he wasn't sure. Good things came to those willing to wait for the right things. There was never anyone more right for him than Cameron.

CHAPTER THIRTY-ONE

Over a year later.

Beautiful people surrounded her. Lucky and her mother looked like Hollywood royalty on the red carpet. Beverly Madden may have turned her back on Hollywood, but as the cameras flashed and the paparazzi called out their names, Cameron knew Hollywood would never forget her mother.

She turned to her right to see Val, who had never looked so handsome. He was always hot in his usual attire of blue jeans and a plaid shirt, but there was something innately sexy about a tuxedo on a man. It was funny to watch him go from the uptight security guard she'd first met to the calm mountain man she'd grown to love and adore. As they made their way into the Dolby Theater, he was back in protector mode.

"Who are you wearing?" reporters called from the sidelines. "What's next for you?" The questions were rapid-fire, but she ignored them all. Her mother had told her to enjoy the moment, and she would. There were little moments to every lifetime, and she didn't want to skip a single one looking for the next big thing when it was already there.

"You look beautiful," Val said as he placed his hand on the

small of her back. "No matter what happens, you deserve to be here."

A year ago, she would have argued with him and told him that connections and birthright got her there, but she'd worked her ass off on *Breakfast with Tiffany*. She'd paid her dues, memorized the script, and delivered the lines. But if Val thought she got there on her own, he was crazy. He'd been there with her every step of the way. He was in every tear she shed, every smile she blazed, and every kiss that touched the hearts of the Academy voters who nominated her for an Oscar. She didn't expect to win. The win wasn't necessary. In her book, she'd won a thousand times over when she and Val stood on the edge of their lake in front of Doc Parker and said I do.

As the evening progressed, she watched her contemporaries celebrate their wins while she counted her blessings. She was a wife, a daughter, and a friend to many. She'd never know who donor #381 was, but she had Lucky, who'd been a father figure all her life. She didn't have a bookstore or a standup mike night, but Val had put a fancy coffee machine in the kitchen and a karaoke machine on the counter with a promise that if she wanted more, he'd build it, and they would come.

The crowd buzzed around her as the nominations for best actress were announced. When the announcer called her name, she smiled. It was every actor's dream to hear their name in that way. She'd come to Aspen Cove looking for something. She thought it was the role of a lifetime, and in a way, it was. She couldn't have been more right or more wrong.

The announcer opened the envelope and pulled out the card. "The Oscar goes to Cameron Madden."

She sat there stunned until Val nudged her to stand and take her place. As she clutched the golden statue, she looked into the audience. Tears streamed down her mother's cheeks, and pride shone in Lucky's eyes, but Val mesmerized her. He didn't care that she was Cameron, the actress. All he cared about was that she was his, and he was hers.

She stared into the audience. "I wasn't prepared to win, so I have only one thing to say." She rubbed her very-pregnant stomach and looked into her husband's eyes. "Never let anyone tell you that you can't have it all." She held the statue in the air. "I love you!"

Up next is One Hundred Desires

OTHER BOOKS BY KELLY COLLINS

One Hundred Desires

GET A FREE BOOK.

Go to www.authorkellycollins.com

ABOUT THE AUTHOR

International bestselling author of more than thirty novels, Kelly Collins writes with the intention of keeping love alive. Always a romantic, she blends real-life events with her vivid imagination to create characters and stories that lovers of contemporary romance, new adult, and romantic suspense will return to again and again.

For More Information
www.authorkellycollins.com
kelly@authorkellycollins.com